Triple No. 4

Angela Woodward
Norman Lock
John Olson

The Ravenna Triple Series
*Chapbooks as they were meant to be read—
in good company.*

Copyright © Ravenna Press, 2017
All rights reserved, reverting on publication to the individual authors

ISBN: 978-0-9985463-4-6

Published by Ravenna Press
USA
ravennapress.com

First Edition

The Language of Birds
  by Angela Woodward   *page*   1

The Cromwell Dixon Stories
  by Norman Lock   *page* 33

Essences and Sentences
  by John Olson   *page* 49

Acknowledgments & Biographies

Angela Woodward

The Language of Birds

"Walter," she said to his sleeping back. "Walter." His breath continued to expand him and deflate him, oblivious to her attention.

*

Almost a dozen of them packed into the elevator with her. Three or four different conversations intersected just above her head, a melodious laugh, somber tones broadcasting an emotional tautness, another laugh like a scarf tossed in the air and floating down languidly, a quiet staccato of information transfer, and their version of "uh huh, uh huh," sputter of confirmation in duet with another musical line. Their intense perfumes mismatched across the enclosed box clanking upwards. She breathed it in deliberately, letting her nostrils fondle the assault. At the fifth floor, the things all jostled out, the last one turning to give her a short bow or nod. The doors approached each other again, two halves sliding towards the central join, the old, calm green of the baroque paint of the hallway becoming slimmer, a sliver, then shut out entirely by the silver slabs. The ride up one more floor by herself did not give her enough time to expand into the space. Instead, the sudden emptiness the things had left pressed into her on all sides. Elizabeth looked up just as the cage slowed, and caught the grid of the ceiling escape hatch, centered exactly over her.

*

"Walter," she said, "I was wondering."
"Oh, were you," he said, his back still to her. His hands sorted through the pile of washers, winking them into categories left right middle. Though she couldn't see his face, she knew its calm blankness, its sealed look as his eyes, cruel masters, oversaw the work of his fingers. Since she'd been working for the things, their evening routine had shifted. They didn't cook or clean anymore, so the apartment had become curiously undemanding, mostly static or easily set back to its starting point. They had worked out a plan when he first got his notice almost a year ago, to steal something from one of the things, which she would seduce with this purpose in mind. Then when he was gone, they could still feel each other, if the thing worked like the rumor had it, that the things possessed a thing that connected flesh to flesh, at a distance. Or they could go at it another way, as Walter preferred a more direct assault, a night attack on a lightly guarded building. Either way, their plan wavered in intensity, at times seeming immensely practical, nothing more than a shopping list, but often faltering into haze, a dimly remembered movie, the actors' faces familiar, the intricacies of the plot forgotten except for that one transcendent scene, the thieves twisting on ropes down

into the treasure chamber in *Topkapi*. "I saw a bunch of things today," she said. "They're all going to that big opera thing."

"Hmm," he said.

"I could get it to take me. You know it offered."

"I thought you already had a plan. I thought you had to go, you know, Step One."

"Are we really doing that?" she said. Though he seemed to be paying no attention to her, she knew he was actually acutely aware of her voice and tone, so much so that he had to temper his perceptions by keeping her behind him. The washers clinked, adding their dry dismay to the conversation.

*

Her hand clicked and circled, while the thing under her gaze widened out, drew back. A quiet ping confirmed successful completion of One A. The things didn't allow them to have coffee or Coke at the stations, though they stocked the kitchenette with all kinds of things, Norwegian and Italian canned fish, tiny cakes in indented plastic platters, dried fruit and ginger, as well as every domestic name brand cracker, Hi Ho, Heigh Ho, Ritz. The demands of the body had to be relegated to that other room, as here the steady light, the smooth surfaces, the paucity of things to touch, let the eyes do their duty undistracted by the other senses. The view continued to expand on screen, another soft ping affirming that One B had been reached. Because it was night there, where the thing she was coordinating was, the colors on the screen drenched out as blue tones, translated from the thing's sensors into tonal variation. If she were there in actuality, where the thing was flying, she wouldn't be able to see anything, because it was dark. But at this immense distance, through the night vision sensors, the leaf canopy etched a mutating pattern, blue on blue. All the edges hardened to pixilated lines, no curves or unexpected humps. The lighter and darker overlay shifting as it flew gave her a sense of sinuous motion.

Early in her training, her trainer had pointed out the shadow of the thing she was flying, thrown onto the landscape it surveyed. It was daytime and desert, so that the shadow's imposition on the uncultivated ground was markedly aberrant. She had taken it for a vehicle or an animal. "Keep looking," her trainer said. "It's an owl," she said. Blood flooded up her neck at her wonder, that she was witnessing its flap and glide at this distance. And it's daylight, she thought. It was returning late from hunting. The owl's adventure unspooled for her, its dive onto the desert rat, the bloody claws, slow, methodical digestion of the meat, expulsion of the bones and hair. The storyline vanished as the trainer laughed. An owl. It's what it had thought itself, before it knew better. Once it had explained that the owl was actually the dark reflection of the thing bumping over the sand below, it looked like exactly that, a wrinkly shadow. The owl flew off into the margin of her mind and had not returned.

*

"Elizabeth," said Walter, pulling her hair into his hands. "We need to find a guy who has grappling hooks, who already knows how to use them."

"Maybe," she said.

"I know one," he said. "I met him at the hospital this afternoon."

"How could that be?"

"Just one of those things, I guess."

"Oh," she said. "You put him under?" She twisted her head to bring her hair back from him, but he reached for it again.

"He'd been prepped upstairs, and they brought him down. I was assisting Dr. Duvaire. I said, you're going to sleep for awhile. It will be the nicest sleep you've ever had. You'll be safe and warm, dreaming, and the whole time, I'll be standing right here, watching over you. Which is what I always say. Count backwards from ten, I told him. By the time you get to seven, you'll be so happy." She closed her eyes, letting him pull her ear to his mouth. "Ten…nine…and just then he told me that he was a thief, skilled with grappling hooks."

"A cat burglar? A jewel thief?" She was almost asleep already, leaning against him.

"Exactly. Just what we need."

*

The dry space behind her eyes softened as the impressions of the evening filled it, a cutting wind on her cheek, the rattling of the leaves in the caged trees along the curb, the preacher at the corner reading from his mystical work: *this servant would not crush even a wilted reed, he would not tread on straw, he would not squeeze a tick or salt a leach. If the hammer were to hit his own thumb and turn it black and throbbing, he would treat his own limb as an innocent baby found in the woods, he would....*

The Cloth of Gold lit its lamps around them. The waitress leaned over and pulled down the blind, shutting them into the brown and green fake forties wall and tabletop. The basketball game, or perhaps last night's basketball game, carried on mutely behind the thing's head. "I'm glad you're here with me," the thing said, radiating its goodwill at her. Even from across the table, she felt too aware of its pungency. She stared at the embroidery visible when its coat fell open. The fanciful lining, blue threads on black silk picking out the outline of a tree or a garden, belied the dull black of the outer layer. The lining vanished when the thing sat back a little, lifting the liquor to its lips. It was the only thing in the restaurant. The other diners had already shivered away from them, hunching their shoulders, hanging their heads, making their bodies slightly narrower so as to increase the distance, decrease the possibility of the thing touching them, or of the thing's voice falling into their ears. As the tiny men on screen battled for the hoop, Elizabeth caught her own eyes in the mirrored back of the bar. Between bottles of Beefeater and Cutty Sark, her turquoise earrings flashed, and a hand swept up to push her hair behind her ears. Her eyes skidded away from her flushed and excited cheeks, and the alluring drop of the top of her top. It hardly looked like her, not at all how she'd looked in the blued glare of the women's bathroom where she had changed from her work clothes into her baring holiday costume.

*

Walter met a man at a bench outside the hospital, where he had gone to smoke. Though he was a nurse and had taken a pledge to live a healthy life, since he'd gotten the notice almost a year ago, he had resumed his former habit to the extent of taking one cigarette occasionally. The wind played ferociously with the match. The man offered the steady flame of his lighter. Then they smoked in silence, turned away from each other. Walter's hospital garb announced his occupation, and more or less his status in life. The man, in baggy brown pants and polo shirt, belonged to the vast category of non-employees, non-staff, non-doctors, either the fodder the hospital worked upon or a relative of same. A van pulled up in the circle drive and began lowering its ramp. Walter shifted his stance so as not to see the old woman descending in her wheelchair, blanket thrown across her lap. A few of the ambulance drivers sputtered out of the parking garage across the road. He didn't know them, and took them in as more character actors in the garage's drama, nameless interchangeable humans that walked in and out of the concrete windpipe.

"You work here?" asked the man on the bench, needlessly.

Walter nodded. He did not ask the man what he was doing. The sun briefly came out from behind the haze that had hidden it. The next car that came up the drive gleamed. The huge revolving door to 3A cast shafts of light off its brass lining. Walter's smoke crossed his face, dulling the air, and when it was gone, the sun too had tucked itself back into its nook. The man on the bench had gotten older, creases around his eyes more pronounced.

*

They went up the walls of the compound at four in the afternoon, as the jewel thief had told them to do. The work day commanded its last stirrings, where the tasks that had been put off since lunch suddenly compelled attention, a quick burst of heads-down precision as the clock hands clicked closer to the moment of release. The equipment Walter had gotten from the man lay neatly wound in his backpack. They hoisted each other up the shed, and from there up the first roof, and along the ridgeline. The things had built them wide, with old stately slate, all stolen from us, Walter said, though Elizabeth had noted before that it had been sold fairly happily, a gleeful commerce that the city still reveled in. The bay stretched itself in a touristy vista. She tapped on his ankle, all she could reach. "Look," she whispered. Twisting his head, he could get only one eye over the bulk of the backpack to focus on her. "Keep going," he said. "But Walter," she said. The slate exhaled its warmth between her knees. Tiny white breaks in the water must have been gulls bobbing on the calm surf. Far out in the distance, the profile of a barge shimmered, as if made of barely coalesced dust.

*

The thing took her hand as they settled into their seats, placing it on top of its knee and squeezing it. It shot her a look of such happiness that she was confused, its even teeth shining a benign joy that lapped her but was not due to her. It released the tension on her hand and she slid it back to herself, but pressed the fabric of its coat as she did so, and so accidentally pulled sideways the giving flesh beneath. It beamed at her again, a softer focus. She felt the blood pour up her neck, shame and excitement mingling.

The thing peeled its coat down and arranged it behind itself, lining the velvet seat with the embroidered silk, column of torso now rising out of billowy folds. All its movements brought its shoulder repeatedly against hers. It wriggled down and came still, lifting the program. "Ah," it said, and conjured reading glasses out of some tuck in the jacket. "Have you ever been there?" it asked her, tapping on an ad for a restaurant, a glass of wine held up against one word in scrolled italics. "No," she said. It settled back to reading, again drawing its shoulder against hers. The heat from this contact slowly amplified, as if a slightly corrosive chemical leaked between them. Each breath brought its scent, too, like another aspect of the thing's animal warmth. She thought, as she often did, of crossing the room to Walter the second time they met, the urgency of her hand closing on his sleeve. Something about the density of his forearm, his intake of breath, had seemed intoxicatingly familiar. "What are you doing?" he said. "I'm sorry," she said. She'd forgotten that they didn't already know each other, that they hadn't already walked the three blocks to Frank's apartment and pressed against each other in the vestibule so that they were almost unclothed before he got the key in the door. Then that scene continued, worn with use to only shapes and forms, clouds of black on black, plumes of underwater ink in the night. Almost she could feel Walter's hands on her still, and his chest under her palms.

The thing was looking at her, head turned slightly, eyes peeking over the rims of the black glasses. It put its hand up, reaching around her head to cup the further ear. It pulled her close and touched its lips to the hair on top of the other ear. It immediately let her go, and she centered again in her seat, looking down at her lap as if nothing had happened. Yet its quick embrace had sent a sensation right down the middle of her brain. Each ear had taken in its touch, and between them a bolt shot down, throat, chest, belly, down, and spread through her perineum, waved, diminished. Elizabeth stifled a cry. She didn't want it to know how it had affected her. But peeping at it, she met its glance, also angled down, indirect, and a tiny twitch of its lip, amused. Had it given her something, or taken something away?

*

Walter had just passed his exams at the hospital when they met, and worked so much that he rarely saw the sun. Up in the dark, home same thing. He gave her a key, and asked her to go to sleep in his bed on the nights Frank was away. He woke her as his legs slid in beside her, never a word, as if Frank was still in the next room, though they were alone. He became a kind of dream pulsation, a night creature condensing out of the dark beneath the blankets and vanishing by dawn. She knew him by touch, and had only a shadowy recollection of his face. His voice on the phone was infrequent. More familiar was his step as he left the apartment, the hesitation at the door, quick walk back to the kitchen to get one more thing, the shuffle into his coat, rattle of the knob as he turned the bolt. From these sounds she inferred the movement of his whole body. One afternoon they had asked her to get some files from another office. All the messengers were busy, and she had volunteered. "Oh, thank you, Elizabeth, you're so good," her then-boss had said, the one who wrote her the reference that got her the thing with the things a few months later. "If that's really what you want," he said. He was old-fashioned, he said, and preferred not to work with the things, though he knew they weren't bad, he wasn't prejudiced, it was just that he didn't quite feel at ease, didn't understand what they were always laughing about. "People say they're content," he said, but he himself considered that they were pleased with themselves, which wasn't the same thing.

"I don't know," she said. "I thought I'd try it." His face pinched in, shutting off the budding remark, that trying things was no good. Released from her duties, the files in hand, all tied in red tape, the literal stuff of the metaphor, and smelling of legality, the afternoon opened up, a pocket of sluggish slothfulness, as her then-boss wouldn't be out of his appointment for another hour. She rode the subway one stop and emerged directly into the hospital lobby. An artificial stream poured down a glass wall, lit by a skylight three stories up, a gigantic open cavern through the middle of the building echoing the soothing roar of water on water. She meant to go to the information desk and page Walter. But she didn't do it. She stood at the lip of the pool, looking down at the silver coins lining the bottom. The money winked up at her, each round catching her eye. She raised her head and saw the flickering golden shadow on the wall behind, the curtain of water remade in light, interrupted by the glittering spots thrown up from the dimes and nickels.

That night she waited up for Walter, and turned the bedside lamp on when he came in. "Look at you!" he said, amazed. She too was amazed at his face, which was so nearly what she remembered him looking like.

*

Walter listened to the man in brown wheeze out his words, the sharp inhale of the cigarette providing punctuation. The man sniffed and twisted the end of his nose, bearing away a bit of snot. He hated the way things were going, he said. He'd seen it all along. If he could stab every damn one of those things on sight, though, he wouldn't do it, he said. It wasn't their fault. They were opportunists, he said, and a long flow of blue smoke formed itself around this word, underlining it and ornamenting it with an asterisk. Opportunists. Walter's cigarette had almost burned itself out, but he kept it between his fingers, close to his face. Threads of gray trickled through the red, the ash gathering and communicating with the burning tobacco, convincing the fire to go out. "I stopped smoking," he said. "I have to bum them now. Do you mind?" The man proffered his pack, not meeting Walter's eyes. He was going in for quite a doozy of an operation, he said.

"Nobody with you?" Walter asked.

"Just me allein," he said. "I've used them all up. I don't care if I never wake up, though." Through the name of the ailment and doctor, Walter deduced that he would be working on the fellow shortly. Walter saw the man in brown briefly as he would be half an hour from now, ID tag around his wrist, smocked in the generic patient's gown, a mound on a cart, the staff talking over him, and not even about him. The murmured names of the instruments and drugs would have more potency than the man. But for now, he cocked his wrist, gesturing with the lit stick. "I know all their weaknesses," he said. "All I wanted to live for was maybe pulling off that job. I had it planned, you know." But it wasn't worth it, he concluded. He didn't care about anything.

Walter looked down the asphalt drive to the apron of the parking garage. More figures trickled across the walkway and vanished into the huge revolving doors. He had three months left before his transfer.

*

"Are we really going to do it?" she asked him.

"It was your idea," he said.

"I know. But I'm not sure I'm serious."

"Do *I* know if you're serious?"

She looked at him. He looked back, appraising. Then she looked at his hand, which was more forgiving than his face. She picked it up and kissed the back of it. She turned it over and slowly drew her lips down into the palm. "I think it's right here," she said. "The thing they have."

"If it was right there, we would have seen it. Everybody would know."

"But it almost works," she said, kissing again the center of his palm.

"You're not doing it right. Stand over there." He directed her to the corner. "Turn around." She faced the wall. Now behind her on the bed, he made no sound. The walls did not reflect him. She thought she felt his eyes on her, but then she wasn't sure. Her skin prickled all along her back. She could almost see herself as he would see her, the line of her spine, but it wasn't really her, only a dim, attenuated version. She had no idea what she looked like from the back. He still made no sound. She didn't know what he was doing. Maybe he wasn't there at all.

"You're sure you didn't feel it?" he asked her again, later, after she got out of the bath.

"Why don't you just not go?" she said. "Then we wouldn't need to do any of this."

"I know," he said. But he'd gotten the notice. He would go, and maybe come back when the tour was up, if all went well.

*

The things were supposed to have a thing that they used to connect to each other, so that they could feel each other at a distance. That's why they were so happy, far from their homes, the crowd of them always laughing in the hallway, calling to each other from opposite sides of the subway tracks, striding down the street arm in arm. Tall, well fed, beautifully dressed in their stunning embroideries, exuding their pampered scents, they seemed to have enough to be happy about even without the alleged thing of theirs. Some said it was implanted just beneath the skin of their palm, others said it was in an almost open wound in the armpit. It could have been hidden in the folds of their sex organs, no one could really say. They could touch their loved one, the one they were bound to, is what most believed, though others said that they could dial anyone up, even one of *them*, meaning someone who wasn't a thing, and do something to them remotely. Hurt someone? Why not? You don't think they're all good, despite their ecstatic music, their grandiose architecture. Full of themselves, that's what they are, and they keep filling themselves with this thing of theirs, wherever it's hidden.

*

As the first notes rose out of the cave in the center of the stage, Elizabeth began to cry. The sounds seemed directly wired to her eyes, the fluttering song transmuting through a predetermined formula and coming out her tear ducts. She was moved, the way a body would move close to a fire if needing warmth, or draw back from one if burnt, a deeply animal reaction with no intervening level of thought or analysis. Black birds spun down from the silver trees, singing to each other over the head of the youth in the cave. Scarves furled off their wings, extending the limbs, so that with each sweep of flight, a black line of calligraphy wrote itself behind them. The double black arabesques carved the yellow stage light, sentences rolling by in strange script, the language of birds. She could almost read it herself, though it was the singing youth who exclaimed his thanks, that since he had drunk the beggar's potion, he was able to decipher the raucous cawing. Don't let it end, she thought, though anxious for the next scene, for the witch's daughter to rise naked from the pool and walk around it, dripping her incantation. The thing beside her pushed against the top of her arm. Its knee leaned into her thigh, but its pressure barely registered. Her attention had vacated her ramparts, and concentrated in the front of her skull.

"You'll enjoy it," the thing had said when it invited her. She wasn't sure. She didn't know anything about the things' music. It was perhaps something only things could like, like they liked so many things, gardens, zoos, pavilions, all their creations stabbed down on top of what had once been shanty neighborhoods and fishing wharves, standing gleaming and triumphant.

*

"Walter, I don't know," she said.

"But we're here already." He leaned back to show her the map he had gotten from the old man, its shaky lines, the exaggerated X for the skylight above the treasure room.

"Count back with me from ten," he said as Dr. Duvaire nodded. The huge cyst in the old man's abdomen had been marked with black pen, though there was no mistaking it. "Ten," Walter said. "You're floating down a wire. Here we go. Nine. Sinking down. The air around you is so warm, can you feel it? How free you are. Eight." *This servant would not crush a withered reed, would not squeeze a burnt-out wick between his fingers. Not the lowliest worm would he tread on, and if he stamped on his own toe, he would feel his flesh to be like a tender child to hold and kiss and feed*....The eyes flickered, an act of will behind them forcing them open against the strong current of the drug Walter pulsed into his veins. You're floating down onto a soft feather mattress, sinking so tenderly, resting, six. But the eyes made one more attempt, pupils dilated, the bright surgical lamp Walter had just begun to pull into focus probably stinging them. It's you, the eyes said. I remember you. Yes, five, said Walter. We talked just a little while ago. But that was another world entirely. Four.

*

The witch's daughter would have killed the young man, but his beauty saved him. She agreed to take him back to her mother's house, where her servants fed him. Elizabeth heard their breath, a massive joint intake as all the things gasped and began to clap and stamp their feet. "What is it?" she whispered as the thing leaned forward. It took no notice of her now, its hands going, floor vibrating, the hall collecting their individual streams of delight and anticipation and aiming these invisible torrents at the center of the stage. To cries of "diva, diva," the witch made her entrance. Now the thing wept, wiping its cheeks with the back of its hand repeatedly. It flashed a glance at her, as if from a passing train that had whipped the thing in one direction while Elizabeth stood on the platform wondering where her ticket was. She smiled forlornly, her cheeks hurting with the artificial stretch. She had thought she was bound up in the music, but clearly, she couldn't enjoy it the way the thing next to her could. Something about how devoted they were, no one else could understand. This hurt her even more, that she was so moved, but by contrast only shallowly. The things all panted for the next glorious melody, their synchronous breath a giant live thing in the auditorium. The singer waited for their silence. Into it she cast a drop, an ink blot, almost a stain, it was so insignificant. The dark point stretched into a line, a rope, into a net she spun effortlessly out into the balcony. It settled around the audience, remarkably catching Elizabeth too.

The golden strands began to saw her body apart. But Elizabeth held still. Surely the singer would put them all back together again after she dismembered them. Her arms fell from her shoulders, legs severed at the thighs, quick, cauterized sensations as the witch sang out her golden wires. Now a strand settled on her shoulder and sliced its way through her ribs. The thing brushed its arm against her, though not looking at her. It was oblivious to her as all the thousands of them leaned into the music, now joined by the young man and the daughter and the chorus of servants. Into the hush of the last note the crowd hurtled its applause, all leaping to their feet, Elizabeth with them. The thing's arm pressed heavy on her, slinging her off balance so that she knocked her head into its neck. It turned to her and again kissed the hair over her ear, awkwardly, elbows out. She turned the other way. Looking out along the aisle, she saw herself again a few seats over, a woman just like her, summer dress, cheeks flushed, hair let go of its clips, hands in motion, the thing next to her radiant, exultant.

*

"What I need you to do is brace your feet, okay?" he said, plying the rope between his hands. They had wheeled the skylight open on its pulley and wrapped the rope and hooks securely around the chimney post. Through the narrow trapezoid, the floor of the treasure room glinted beneath, only the portion directly under the skylight visible, rest of the room borderless, undefined. The moon had risen in front of them as the sun set behind. The white disk looked on, coolly curious, while the red orb sizzled into the bay. She could only see its alarmed face if she looked over her shoulder. She kept her eyes on the moon's more indifferent expression. Pigeons called, rasping their feet against the tin gutters, as Walter whispered his instructions.

"We should both go down," she interrupted. "I'll take the other rope."

"I set it up like this," he said.

"I know," she said. "But we have to change it. I don't want to wait up here. It will take two of us, one to lift the glass, one to take the thing."

"No," he said. "Don't be ridiculous. It works this way."

"Walter," she said. He kept turned from her, so he couldn't translate all the after-effects she put into his name. Because of his angle, her word bounced off him and hit her in the throat, coming back imbued with a deep tiresomeness—he doesn't care for me, he stopped some time ago, he's a stranger. "Walter," she said again, aiming it lower.

"It'll be all right," he said, looking full at her, neck twisted. He tugged the rope sharply. "See?" She did see the lines of his arms, his grace and concentration, the shadow the moon made on his cheeks, and the underlying burden of his feeling for her.

*

It followed her into the kitchen the next day. She chanced to get something to eat when she thought she saw it go into the conference room with the others. But it must have been alert to her movement, the vacated desk calling to it. It didn't say anything or touch her, merely fiddled with the hot milk thing on the fancy espresso machine. As foam began to spout into the cup, it looked over at her, thoughtful, slightly wounded, wondering. "They'd cut off your hair if they knew," it said softly.

She took some of the exquisite deli meat out of its plastic wrapping. They fed them without limit, all sorts of things, the kitchen endlessly restocked.

"You know I'm discreet," it said. "I'll look after you."

"Leave me alone," she said, mouth full of sandwich.

It turned such a look on her she was immediately stricken. They were always so happy, she had no idea they could be hurt. It looked at her just like Walter, face muscles rigid, battlements firm, while hurt poured out its eyes. "I'm just a plaything?" it said. "Something like that?"

The witch's daughter had showed the young man her most precious possession: King Solomon's ring. With it on one finger, she could fly. On another, she could burst rock. Wearing it on another finger, it turned her invisible. As long as he held onto her, he could do all these things with her. And so they made love in the middle of the market place, the ring hiding them from the streams of singing, dancing folk. As she closed her eyes in passion, he slipped the ring onto his own finger and flew away from her. Now he meant to kill the dragon that oppressed his land. The witch, finding that her daughter had lost the valuable ring, turned her into an eagle and banished her to a mountaintop.

"Stop," she meant to say as the thing reached into her shirt in the back of the cab. But it was all she could do to suppress her moan as it released something so tender in her. It drew back, and ran its fingertips along her cheek, barely touching. The young man faced the dragon bravely, using the ring to fling boulders at it. But the beast opened its mouth and swallowed him, ring and all. The eagle, flying over, sang her lament for her lost love. He betrayed me. He stole from me, when I would have given it to him willingly. Because he understood the language of birds, this forlorn crowing came to him as intelligible speech. "Save me now," he cried. "I don't deserve it. But I beg you, kill the dragon and release me." The audience held vastly quiet, a thousand delayed exhales, then their hushed weeping to accompany the last duet. Elizabeth felt her eyes overflow, the music manipulating her body, opening taps, adjusting settings, loosening stitching, reassembling parts. "We can feel the same things," the thing said, speaking only through its fingertips. "Do you want it?"

*

She locked her legs against the solid chimney as Walter disappeared through the skylight. The sound of the guard's footsteps rang up, softer now as it went the other way, making its loop away from them. The lights behind her picked out the rectangle of pier disappearing into the bay some miles away, while a red speck moved across the water, the retreat of an invisible boat. Overhead, the moon continued its calm consideration, judging her posture, her forehead and hair, and perhaps her intentions too, the treacherous, contradictory thoughts. The rope spun slowly against the pulley, letting out evenly as Walter descended into the chamber. She could see nothing of him, and the rope appeared unchanged, the slim white line against the dark window the same even as it lengthened. Though the rope in her hands connected them fiber to fiber, she didn't know what he was thinking. In fact he was completely gone to her, the old man's diagram stitched across his brain while she leaned into the thing's embrace, that same sense as at the climax of the music, that she curled and uncurled as directed by the sound, frictionless unwinding into the scented flesh of the thing, not at all alien and already a part of her. "Ah," it said, touching her throat, unless it was her who had spoken.

*

"I thought I heard you come in," he said, squinting at her, eyes puffy with sleep, as she dried herself off. "You took a shower?"

She pulled the curtain shut again so it wouldn't mildew.

"Did you find anything out?"

"I'll tell you tomorrow," she said. "I'm tired."

"Well, was it at least interesting? What was it like?"

"I can't explain," she said.

"You could try."

"No," she said. "You have to be up in two hours. Why don't you go back to bed?"

He took a step back from her, then hovered at the door. As she pulled open the medicine cabinet, his face came closer to her in the mirrored door. The dense water droplets obscured his expression.

"I've got the thing," she said. "It gave it to me right away."

"It gave you the thing?"

"Here," she said, showing him the bead in the tip of her index finger.

"Does it work?"

"No," she said. "I've been trying to wake you for hours. You didn't feel it. Didn't move."

"It's my fault, then?"

She closed the cabinet. The steam slid down it, cutting his reflection into strips. The whole, however, was in its way as it had ever been.

*

The rope checked against her palm, a shudder of stopped tension. She reeled it back up a few inches until another tug came, enough. Now he would be lifting the top off the glass cabinet, evading the multiple sensors by swooping down so gently from above. The floor, dissected by motion-detectors, remained lulled, the walls untouched, the alarms surrounding the treasure case unrung. The thing, embedded in a jewelled dagger they had brought from their distant homeland, allowed the things to embrace each other at a distance. At their annual ceremony, they inoculated each other with it, glorious interconnectivity that fed their boastful, unceasing happiness. "We are one," read their flag, that snapped even now in the night wind. The footsteps of the circulating guard came nearer, coming just past the furthest point on its route. The rope shuddered again. She let it out, then urgently up, the other way. The pulley whined. Walter had oiled it, but the moist air from the bay had already stiffened it, or some inner, unlubricated part was now in play. She pulled, staggering to her feet, leaning back against the chimney for leverage. A scrap of cloud drew across the moon's face. It disapproved so much that it wouldn't watch the outcome. The footsteps continued their measured increase in volume, drumming in ostinato to the screech, screech of the pulley. Walter's head came up, then shoulders, then flailing arms. She ran towards him, regardless of the rope. It spun out of her hands, and he scrabbled at the lip of the skylight. "Did you get it?" she whispered. His arm clapped along the slate, slapping something down. She grabbed at him to pull him to safety, but couldn't get him up beyond his waist. The hooks and webbing clawed into the underside of the skylight. He held himself up by one arm, the other reaching down to undo the tangled equipment. He fell back onto the slate, now free, sending a shingle skidding towards the gutter. Elizabeth blocked it with her foot, deflecting it but not stopping its slide. With a loud coo and flap, a pigeon flew up and banged into the open lid of the skylight. Its form traced itself gray against black, a smudge like a comma disappearing into the gap. They heard the wind of its wings, the booming, startled flutter below, and then the voice of the alarm as the bird rocked the glass case.

*

When he first got his notice almost a year ago, they started planning a way to steal the thing that would allow them to feel each other at a distance, even after he was gone. The things were said to possess a thing that connected them to flesh to flesh, so a touch of their own skin brought them into contact with the skin of their lover. Walter, going to sleep in his other part of the world, would leave her with a kiss, and when she woke alone and thought of him, she would put her hand on his neck. In the evenings they laid out steps, One A,

One B, revolving and rotating their requirements. She thought she could seduce one of the things, who were notorious for their sensuality. Or if he preferred a more direct attack, they'd go after it in their stronghold, circling down into it like the thieves in *Topkapi*. Their plan wavered in intensity, at times seeming immensely practical, nothing more than a shopping list, but often faltering into a worn topic of conversation, a rutted track that kept them side by side while their minds wandered into separate alleys they kept closed off from each other.

"Walter," she said to his sleeping back. "Walter." His breath continued to expand him and deflate him, oblivious to her attention.

*

Her hand clicked and circled, while the thing under her gaze widened out, drew back. A quiet ping confirmed successful completion of One A, securing the thing on the runway. She moved its levers, fingers tapping, the sound of the keyboard muffled by the gray, absorbent partitions. Her view into the screen sent her eyes through the cameras of the thing. Even as it ascended and surveyed its blue-on-blue canopy of trees, her sense of scale remained the same, bound by the borders of the display. She typed in the codes and clicked on the tags as they flickered up in their green squares in the upper right, lower right. The things wouldn't tell them where anything was, the coordinates encoded, and the colors, bleached through the night vision sensors, blurring the distinction between daylight and dark. It was possible the thing she manipulated launched from a shaft in the next building, or from a suburban silo within the same time zone. More likely her actions involved her in the things' conquest of some other distant landscape. Possibly, she had heard, the things that filled her days were only tests and simulations, staged re-enactments of past or putative flights. Her intense scouting for aberrations—the shadow on the ground, the blurs and clouds that sometimes asked for her attention—only confirmed scenes already known and mapped.

As her eyes drew into the pixilated view, the back of her mind, left untended, went off in its own direction. Although he'd left months ago, Walter's arm across her hip, his breath against her shoulder, replayed as vividly as ever, while overheard words wove another strand, *this servant would not break a withered reed, would not crush a flea that bit his arm. Even the hangnail bleeding off his thumb he would love as his own child, so tender is this servant....* Despite the blunting insulation from sound, the heating and cooling ducts whispered, the conference room doors thudded, and from all sides rose the muffled staccato of keyboards and mice. "Walter," she said. "Wake up, Walter." She pressed the bead in her finger to her lips. Across the far window, sliced into bars by the vertical blinds, a shape passed, quick black against the blue, a crow diving from tree to wire. "Walter," she said. "I'm here." She clicked the next box, and the viewer zoomed back as the thing gained height. Its shadow coursed with them, bent, shriveled, browned out, this caricature of a winged body over the surveyed ground. Insubstantial, with no force to bend the grass, nevertheless it might have caused a slight coldness on the ground in its path, or made creatures it touched look up momentarily.

Norman Lock

The Cromwell Dixon Stories

for Brian Evenson

Contents

1. In Envy of Glaciers, 35
2. The Havoc of the Stars, 37
3. Semiotics and the Dragon, 39
4. The Universe of the Body, 41
5. The Disappearances, 43
6. Explodoing Heads, 45
7. Crossing into Night, 47

1. *In Envy of Glaciers*

Cromwell Dixon shut his eyes and opened them and was amazed how much time had passed unnoticed in dreamless sleep. Amazed, then suddenly frightened at the fierce velocity of it: time, that swift courier of the Absolute. "This will never do," he told himself and swore to forego postprandial napping and keep more waking hours than had, till now, been his custom. "It is the drink," he thought, twiddling nervously a swizzle stick. "Strong drink is robbing me of time," he said sipping his martini. But he could not slake his thirst; could not resist that alcoholic happiness.

He poured another—this a single malt, for "purity" —and put his feet up on the stool and resumed his old anxiety that time would not stand still. He would have been content had it crawled a while, even ambled— anything but this racing unto—he would not say the word. Then, swigging twice "for courage," said it: "Death," aloud. The word astonished the silence like a glass splinter. If only he could live a stone's life: enter geologic time described by Lyell, whom Cromwell knew from public television. He went into the backyard and caressed some rocks, then sighed at the rocks' impassivity and considered that a rock's minute consciousness is too boring to distract one from the awful contemplation of eternity: endless time being as terrifying to him as its opposite. Rather, he thought, a glacier—that's the thing! Cromwell could easily imagine a glacier's life, entirely happy and self-possessed as it moves 3 feet a day down the austere valley, entertaining thoughts of the temperate plains below and the eventual sea. Cromwell did the arithmetic with pencil and paper, in despite of technology (his wife had a calculator)—figured 3 ft. per day is .125 ft. per hour is .00002 miles per hour. At such a rate consciousness would slow, slow, but not extinguish. The world would make a slight impression on his icy calm, his stately progress toward a distant (therefore welcome) dissolution. He would have time to think and dream and watch the clouds swan across the sky without terror.

Unnoticed, night had crept into the yard and with it a chill harbinger of winter. Shivering, Cromwell turned his collar up and hurried into the house.

2. *The Havoc of the Stars*

Circling the dark cul de sac with his dog, Cromwell Dixon fled precipitately the stars, suddenly afraid of what their ancient light might do to the sensitive precincts of his inner eye. "It must have some effect," he reasoned, tripping over a pavement slab lifted malevolently by a maple root. Starlight cannot help but carry baggy remnants from the Era of Inflation, that one-trillionth of a second after the Big Bang. Good God, ylem (the primal goo announced by Gamow) may even cling to its red shift! And what weariness having traveled so far, so fast from remotest space-time to be caught in Cromwell's eyes! He closed them tight and saw on the black screen of his shut lids the empty beam of time's recession. Fearing an accelerated biological clock, he hurried home, head down, dragging his complaining bitch behind.

A copy of *The Scientific American* left mysteriously in Cromwell's mailbox, claiming in a typewritten note to have come "From a Friend," had increased an anxiety already inflamed by Singularities—rips in the universal fabric where all known physics falter. (Such a friend!) "As if background radiation or Absolute Zero isn't upsetting enough!" he screamed at his wife. Alarmed by Cromwell's morbid sensibility, she blackened thereafter all announcements of dangerous educational TV programming; intercepted and censored papers and magazines for potentially disturbing news. "Come away from the window," she said, "and forget Lemaitre's gigantic rushing chandeliers." But he could not, convinced of the havoc of the stars.

He did pour a drink, finding its liquid light less ominous than stellar rarefaction. Martini in hand, Cromwell ascended the stairs, Mrs. Dixon having gone ahead to turn down the sheets and draw the blinds (to keep out the prying eyes of stars and of the voyeur across the driveway whose astronomy embraced bedrooms). Head spongy with ylem, Cromwell lay down and sipped martini while she undid the buttons of her blouse. Studying a cobweb trapeze at play on the ceiling, he remembered how, in 1907, his namesake had traversed the Cincinnati sky in a breast-shaped balloon. "Oh, fortunate man," thought Cromwell as the lights went out and his wife creaked into bed, "to have been ignorant of all the century had in store!" He signed and allowed himself to be consoled for having such a sensitive nature, such an inquiring mind.

The dog, which had leapt after Cromwell into bed, threw up.

3. *Semiotics and the Dragon*

Cromwell Dixon put the water on for tea. His wife was sick. Her hair hurt, she said. He made toast and, taking the piping hot pot off the gas ring, made tea with lemon. He went outside for the newspaper and returned with a dragon. He delivered breakfast and the paper to his wife upstairs, whose hair was feeling better but whose teeth now hurt. "Someone has left us a dragon in a box," he told her. "There was no note." "You've been drinking again, Cromwell," she said wearily, because of her illness and her husband's intemperance. Cromwell shrugged indifferently and went downstairs "to tend the dragon," which must too, he thought, have needs.

But what are a dragon's needs? Of reptiles he knew nothing, except for 5&10-cent store turtles, which died, inevitably, of some mysterious blight to their pretty green shells. (Mysterious to him!) But dragons? Emblematic dragons such as those inhabiting Medieval English Literature or, on obscure holidays, the streets of Chinatown—Cromwell knew, though not (he would be the first to admit) their archetypal meaning. "Ours is a civilization that has no use for dragons," he thought.

Although he liked to pretend otherwise, Cromwell was a man for whom the things of the world could not truly be said to exist until he read about them, or saw them on educational TV. And so, returning the dragon to its box, he decided to research the thing itself—the quiddity of dragon, paying special attention to its appetites. "I'm off to the library!" he shouted upstairs to his wife, who sighed, knowing that Cromwell's trips to the library were often occasions for libation.

Cromwell searched the shelves. He refused to use the electronic catalogue, missing the wooden cabinets whose drawers filled with index cards had comforted him with the weight of intellectual history. But he never found a book on dragons. He went home, instead, with one on semiotics. So the universe is constructed of sentences! (He had thought all along that this might be the case.) Without them no one could name its parts or establish any relationship among them. For the man without language, the aphasiac, the universe is inscrutable. A gaggle of discrete phenomena. ("Gaggle?" Yes! All muddle and noise.) In the beginning, the Word. Before that, Chaos. Without sentences, nothing. (At least nothing intelligible.)

At home he pronounced "Dragon" over the dragon that stood stiffly, exhibiting a saurian stillness. "You are a dragon," he told it. "Your sentence is related to my sentence by a variety of verbs: to find, to see, to hold, to ponder. Engaging you in language, I make you be." (What? An embodiment of myth, or a mythic representation of the real, or an image on a bottle of Chinese beer.) Upstairs, his wife was dissolving into nothingness under the rumpled sheet of the sickbed now that Cromwell was no longer forming sentences about her. But the dragon—the Dragon was roaring.

4. *The Universe of the Body*

Cromwell Dixon flung out his arms against the chenille bedspread and waggled his fingers at the remote edges of the known universe. Eyes closed, he felt the solar wind, the grit of original dust—felt the light streaming against his skin. "Consciousness and the universe are one and the same," he said to himself, for who else was there to listen? "For everyone, a different universe. What each one knows defines the extent of the universe for him, or her, or it"—thinking of his dragon, which was by now a household pet, having lost its mystery. His mind, usually so probing, so questing, was sailing back to a much earlier time when his entire world lay precisely at his fingertips, was (he smiled) a breast. He had been flipping back and forth earlier between a TV program on Hubbell Deep Field Research and the History of Lingerie. Both held him spellbound. Exhausted by the effort to view them simultaneously, he was now in bed, meditating on the pleasures of a universe of the body.

Then chocolate, and the earthly paradise in the dream town of Tulla where the cahuaquahitl grows, visited by multi-colored birds. Quetzacoalt had brought the cocoa tree there from the sacred fields of the sun. The sun, which was cooling. The sun, which had only four billion years left to shine upon the cahuaquahitl and Cromwell. Quetzacoalt had also brought the people of

Tulla astronomy. It was astronomy that had led Cromwell to chocolate—in his mind. He did not like chocolate. He liked gin. He liked beer and anchovy sandwiches. Not sweets! He also liked lingerie. Some reminded him of bonbons wrapped in crinkly pastel papers. He let his mind go. But no farther than the universe, which stopped at the moment just beyond his fingers picking at the tufts of chenille.

"A universe of the body," he thought languidly. "How comforting for a mind that is tormented by the uncertainty of quarks, by body-piercing neutrinos and the Ultraviolet Catastrophe. By String Theory!"

His wife battered down the door. (Or so it seemed to Cromwell in his drowse.) She italicized the silence, she havocked! (He felt perfectly free to unhinge syntax.) "What are you up to in the middle of the afternoon?" she demanded. "Get up—the hedges need trimming!" "And what of the cahuaquahitl?" he asked. "Do jeweled birds still sing in its branches?" "Drunk again!" she scolded as she took herself out of the room, beyond the sweet smell of the cocoa tree, before Cromwell could reach for her and—speaking tender words of astronomy—show her his stars in the dream city of Tulla.

5. *The Disappearances*

The first street to disappear went unnoticed. Of the city's inhabitants (twenty-thousand souls!), only Mrs. Santos, who rented a house in the middle of the block, complained to the Department of Streets. If she had not gone to the fish market that morning, she, too, would most certainly have vanished. Her husband's passion for halibut saved her. Less fortunate, Mr. Santos disappeared together with his neighbors and a pumpkin-colored dog asleep under the porch. The Director of Streets shrugged and would not commit himself. "It is our responsibility to keep our city's streets in good repair," he said. "Missing persons are outside our jurisdiction. I suggest you talk to the Missing Persons Bureau." Turning his back dismissively on Mrs. Santos, the Director of Streets returned to his pepper and egg sandwich.

She went to the Missing Persons Bureau. "Our interest lies in missing persons," the Director said, "not in missing streets." Mrs. Santos remarked the persons of that street were missing along with the street, but he was not convinced.

Cromwell Dixon touched her elbow and nodded towards the door. She understood that he wanted to have a word with her and went out into the hall. "What do you want?" she asked. "It's an illusion," he replied. "What is?" She raised an eyebrow suspiciously. "The streets are not really disappearing," he assured her. "But my husband …?" "Is home asleep in bed." She looked at Cromwell as if he were crazy. "Come and see," he said, taking her arm.

They walked into an empty field. "See?" she said. "No street, no house, no husband." Cromwell, who had been through this before, began to choke her until, with a gasp, she woke up next to her husband in bed. "I had a funny dream," she wheezed, "about that crazy man whose house I clean." "Who, the bald-headed one who drinks?" "Mr. Dixon," she nodded. "He's nuts!" he said. "A funny dream," she repeated; but she went to the window and looked at the street just in case. "Get me a piece of halibut tomorrow," her husband said as he rolled over and fell back to sleep.

6. *Exploding Heads*

Cromwell Dixon hurried into the bathroom for a painkiller. He felt as if his head were about to explode. Heads, he knew, were exploding in Saõ Paulo, unaccountably, like hot light bulbs struck by cold rain. He had read about them— those heads—while standing in the supermarket checkout line. He had never been to Saõ Paulo, but he knew from Oliver Sacks that encephalitic diseases could spring up here and there "like brush fires" without an agency of contagion. Cromwell was convinced there was something wrong with his brain. He took his temperature; but by the time he could distinguish the level of mercury in the glass tube, it may have cooled. Most probably had. Tomorrow he would buy a digital model. Hopefully, his brain would last through the night.

"Sleep," he told himself, "sleep that knits up the raveled sleeve of care." That from Hamlet, whom Cromwell had played one weekend for the dramatic society. "With the intensity of a slug," one critic quipped. Slugs. Who knew exactly the intensity of a slug? Might not a slug be ardent, in its way? A hand grenade seems listless, too, until the pin is pulled, then "Bang!" And with that bang, Cromwell remembered his own quite possibly imminent detonation.

He poured a large one, and another—to get a start on unconsciousness—then went to bed, nodding on the way to his wife, who sat curled up on the couch like a big ball of wool. (Pink wool, and yellow for her hair.) "I have a headache," he said softly, his hand elegant on the newel post. "Do you want a vinegar compress?" she asked solicitously. "No, no …" he replied, for he knew his condition was too grave for compresses. He threw her a kiss—who knows, perhaps the last—and dragged himself up the stairs.

He closed his eyes; and the bed drifted off into the dark space behind them, drifted into sleep's black ocean—to Saõ Paulo where heads were exploding in the dark like light bulbs.

7. *Crossing into Night*

Cromwell Dixon sat in his backyard and thought. If God exists, would he want Him for a neighbor? Would Cromwell invite Him fishing or for cocktails to ease the coming of the night? Cromwell shook such thoughts out of his head: the Almighty in a rowboat! The Ancient of Days prescribing the perfect martini! Cromwell wasn't interested. He counted pigeons on a wire instead and wondered about a pigeon's mental processes while night descended. "No more of that!" he said, tired at last of looking into the spreading dark.

He took stock of his world: the house whose windows threw yellow oblongs on the grass. A birdbath brimming with autumn leaves. Six pigeons on a wire thinking the thoughts of their kind. His wife opened an upstairs window and shook the dust out of a rag. The pigeons flew, making a disgruntled noise. And the black wire—so he imagined—trembled, obedient to one of Newton's laws.

Newton, too, had sat and thought. Cromwell had not read the great *Principia*; but certain he was that Newton would relish a cocktail now and again when his eyes bleared with equations, would like to feel the tug of an invisible flounder on the line.

Cromwell shut his eyes and opened them and wondered whether he did not possess a second eyelid which, open at last, might show him what until that moment had remained invisible: the reason for all things. The hidden wire. The light inside the feather light as air. If he could find it, that lid. If he could just. Enough! He shook his head to empty it and ate the bloodshot olive that had been peering at him from out the depths of his martini. And then Cromwell Dixon drank and was happy for having crossed, once more, the bridge into night without stumbling.

John Olson

Essences and Sentences

for Roberta

Contents

Structure as a Drunken Seed of Collar Studs, 51
On Getting Old, 55
A Little Attitude, 58
On Knowledge, 63
Directions, 67
Metaphysics as a Form of Jungle Gym, 70
The Matter of the Balcony Railing, 73
Ragwort and Rattlepod, 74
Sillybrations, 80
Aerial Ikebana, 83
Essences and Sentences. 90
Walking and Dancing, 94
Moss, 95
Ruskin and Rust, 96
Intervals, 98
Song Brocade, 103
Tinfoil, 106

Structure as a Drunken Seed of Collar Studs

I like to think about structure. The airplane has a structure that allows it to fly. The gun has a structure that allows it to fire a bullet. Veins have a structure that allows blood to circulate through the body. Blood has a structure that allows it to carry oxygen to the cells of the body.

The body is full of structure. Arms, legs, feet, hands, fingers, genitals, bones, cartilage, skin.

The head has a structure that renders it ideal for the storage and maintenance of the brain, the attachment of ears and nose and eyes and the disposition of a mouth.

The mouth has a structure, a tongue, a palate, a pair of lips. These structures permit the mouth to make meaningful sounds called words which are put together in a structure called a sentence.

I can think about structure all day. It's fun to think about structure. The world is in chaos. Structure is reassuring.

Structure is essentially a matter of inter-related elements organized in such a way as to create a purpose, an identity, or a pearl. Most of these items are referred to as objects. Not all objects are objects.

Is a quark an object? Yes and no. The quark is an elementary particle with certain demonstrable properties such as electric charge, mass, color charge and spin. There are six types of quarks which are identified as flavors: up, down, strange, charm, top, and bottom.

A quark, however, is not an object like a fire extinguisher or parking meter. It doesn't have an architecture like a church or library but it does experience all four fundamental interactions: electromagnetism, gravitation, strong interaction and weak interaction.

What I'm currently writing is a strong interaction. Your interest in what I'm writing may be either a strong or weak interaction.

The structure of this thought is long and simultaneous and looks like a propeller.

The meaning of a complex expression is determined by its structure and the meanings of its constituent elements.

I try picking up a spider on the bedroom wall. He takes off as soon as I touch one of his impossibly thin legs. Or is it a she? Should I wash my hands after touching a spider even though I barely touched it? What's so dirty about a spider? If the spider has venom in it (which I'm sure that this one didn't) doesn't it have to bite you to get the venom into you?

"I could've given less matter a better ear," says Pompey in Act II scene 1 of Shakespeare's *Antony and Cleopatra*.

What is matter, and does matter matter?

Matter is anything composed of atoms and has mass and interaction energies. All the objects we encounter in life is a form of matter. This matters. This is a matter that may be described as a light bulb or farm.

A farm of words. I'm farming words. I'm farming a form of words. I'm forming a farm of words.

These words may be observable as physical objects. It all depends on atoms.

There are atoms in your eyes and atoms in your nerves.

For example, if a brush invites hair, a locomotive will become amber and triumph in credibility. The goal of soda is not to quench thirst but modify the meaning of clay. The formula for meringue displays a reckless appreciation of collar studs. All sentences are events. The garden traffics in seeds and annuls declension with a breeze, although the breeze comes from elsewhere and isn't an intrinsic feature of the garden, a movement of air is fundamental to the garden that is the sentence.

The oak holds green in its leaves and the night accommodates the journeys of the moon. Beehives chronicle the elegance of reproduction. Kerosene thrusts its calypsos at a page of overweening science. The result is swampy.

Why am I feeling so metallic today? It's as if I had something to declare but don't know what it is. I feel an urgency to express something ineffable.

Does that have structure? Not really.

Structure is one of the privileges of cognition. Sooner or later, everything comes to a boil. One might ponder somersaults and bingo! you discover the mobility of paint. As for me, I prefer Boston clam chowder to Manhattan clam chowder. I like collecting shellfish and providing reasons for the use of gravel. Have you ever seen a philodendron do cartwheels?

The human shoulder is a magnificent piece of engineering. The humerus connects to the scapula like a ball and socket. This permits sobbing, harmonica playing, and the movement of furniture.

You can shake yourself free of languor and fish for sturgeon. I recommend the Black Sea. The sturgeon there are big. The sturgeon there are reduced in number by overfishing and poaching. So forget what I said. Don't fish for sturgeon in the Black Sea.

Study structure.

The structure of seeds. The structure of inebriation. The structure of maturity.

Black man driving a pink Eldorado down Boren. We are both stopped at the intersection of Boren and Pike. His top is down and he is bald. Brahms 15th symphony is playing on his radio. The word 'Eldorado' is lettered in chrome. The word is broken. The front part says 'Eldor' and hangs down. 'aldo' is horizontal. That is its structure.

I'm musing on something I saw earlier in the day: a silver Honda Civic parked on the curve of 8th Avenue West. All four tires were missing. A bumper sticker said "Cattitude."

Do you see how structure works? Particle and wave. Succotash and Brahms.

On Getting Old

Existence accumulates like alluvial deposits in a river. Disillusionments, humiliations, hallucinations, manias, aversions, conflicts, chaos, rocks.

Wrinkles don't help. Beauty belongs to the young. And we all know how that goes.

Do I feel differently now than I did when I was twenty? Yes and no. Some things change. Some things do not. The things that change are mostly body related. It takes longer to heal. It's harder to get up from a chair. I have to learn how to urinate all over again because an enlarged prostate demands patience. Women have their problems, too. Menopause. That can't be fun.

What're you going to do?

You adapt. You don't have a choice. You're on a raft. You're being carried down a river. There are rapids ahead. You get through the rapids. The water gets still. Then you hear a roar. Is that a roar or a hiss? Is that the wind in the trees or something else? Something scary, like a waterfall. Oh shit, you think, there's a waterfall ahead.

You don't appreciate being young when you're young. How can you? When you're young you're young. The bones are forgiving. The muscles are limber. The skin is supple. Innocence is an embarrassment you're eager to be rid of.

It's because I'm old that I get to speak in generalizations like this. I was young once and I didn't feel like this. This takes time.

You need to get old in order to feel young. Why is that? Because when you're young you're too inexperienced to know anything else. You can't feel young if you don't know what it is to be young. When you're old, you definitely know what it is to be young. Those sensations don't go away. Where would they go? They become a part of you. They inform you. They school you. They feed you.

La vieillesse est aussi le moment de goûter le fait d'être en vie comme un bien inestimable, et au fur et à mesure que je me rapproche vraiment de la mort, je goûte la vie comme jamais je ne l'ai goûtée, observes 94 year old French philosopher Marcel Conche. "Old age is additionally the moment of tasting the experience of being alive as an inestimable good, and as I gradually and unequivocally approach death, I taste life like I've never tasted it before."

The older I get the more I need a camel. I have a hunger to see the stars. The afternoon lifts itself into my eyes and I realize there is a limit to life but there's also the flavor of nothingness to consider, the lure of oblivion, the excitement of murdering distance with Switzerland.

We inherit the decisions of our youth. That's the sad part. Or was that supposed to be the good part? I made crazy decision in my youth. No need to go into that now. Suffice it to say, the man who sits here now once read passages of *The Iliad* in front of a crematorium during breaks as a factotum in a funeral home.

What happened to that guy? Is that guy still within me? Yes, but he has since retired. He now reads Proust in

French at an old brown desk and gets invitations to be cremated in the mail.

He has widened his embrace of the universe. He can smell the fourth dimension.

Think about artichokes. How multilayered they are. The older one becomes, the more multilayered one becomes. Leaf upon leaf upon leaf upon leaf. Youth is the stubborn stuff at the heart.

I drink my coffee from a Beatles mug. The Beatles never age. Their songs sound fresh every time I hear them. I've heard every song at least thousands of times. They age. They get better. I look at John. I look at George. It seems unreal that they don't exist.

We are in the realm of the immediate. No ideas but in things.

Time imitates the movement of stars.

The snowman in Zen philosophy is a symbol of the nothingness that is at the core of Being. I find youth in snow. We must learn to imitate the nothingness of snow.

I find it interesting that we need permission for certain things. We all carry with us a set of borders, a sense of what is acceptable and what is unacceptable. This is what makes you old.

You can learn a lot from sugar. It was while waiting for a cube of sugar to dissolve in a glass of water that Henri Bergson learned the true nature of life, duration, and time. He learned that our conception of time is an artificial construct.   Experience is an active process.

Categories are a just form of shorthand. We need them for basic communication.

Creativity is protean. Nothing is ever quite as real as the present moment. It is in the present moment where time is water and our minds are sugar. Dissolution is the start of something new. Each moment is a creative act. And so, from hour to hour, we ripe and ripe, and then, from hour to hour, we rot and rot; and thereby hangs a tale.

A Little Attitude

It's difficult to imagine a time before coffee. When did I begin drinking it? When was the first morning in which I got up and made myself a cup? Why do I have no memory of it?

Coffee is indispensable. I won't say it's as vital as blood, but it's in the same neighborhood. It occupies a realm somewhere between deerskin and perforation.

Without coffee, morning would be dry as algebra. There are some things that render life more palatable. Coffee is one of them. I know it's not good for anxiety. It makes it worse. But it makes it worse in a good way. It gives it an edge. It gives it a Dutch uncle. A rip saw and a rite of passage.

Coffee will not be the same for everybody. It's a little like marijuana in that respect. I never liked marijuana. It makes me paranoid. But a lot of people do like marijuana. You can see it in their faces. Joy. Dahlias and herbivores. But not me. Me, I cower in a corner waiting for the Swat Team.

I like beginning my day with something dark and a little bitter. It suits my temperament. It gives me attitude. Attitude is everything. In the dynamics of flight, attitude refers to the orientation of a vehicle around its center of mass. Coffee helps me get oriented in three-dimensional space.

I love the smell of coffee. It's the smell of writing. It's the smell of enhancement. Concentration, conversation, home. Coffee is good for the intellect but eventually I get the urge to do something physical. My legs are worn. I know I should take a day off but I can't. I have to go for a run. If I don't I feel like shit. But what if I cause further injury? What if I fuck things up so badly I have to take months off from running?

I decide to give yoga a shot. I follow the routine of a young woman on YouTube. In the yoga tradition there are names for all the poses she demonstrates. I do a table, a cat, a cow, a sunbird, a child and a plank. I stretch my right arm while stretching my left leg. I stretch my left arm while stretching my right leg. I lift my torso and pedal the floor. I bring my hands together in prayer and let them down like the scattering of butterflies. Thirty minutes later I feel nausea. I feel seasick. I tap the screen of my Android tablet and the woman stops issuing instructions and moving gracefully into postures that perplex and discombobulate my body. I wish life were like that. Tap a screen and make things stop.

I decide yoga is not for me.

The next day I decide to get back into my running. But before I go anywhere I have to wait for the delivery of a new washing machine. The delivery is scheduled between 10:00 and 11:30 a.m.

Two huge men arrive at 10:45. Just one arrives first. The other guy stays in the truck. I lead the man down to the laundry room. Our building has an entry with a slate floor and a flight of steps that go up and a flight of steps that go down. The laundry room, which is small with a linoleum floor, is at the bottom. The man moves the old washer out and clamps his pliers on the hose coupling. It won't budge. This worries me. The man adds to my worry by telling me that if he can't get it off they can't deliver the new washer. It's company policy. It protects them from costly plumbing repairs if the pipe should burst. This is bad news. The washer serves four units. We've all got dirty clothes piling up. He gives it another firm twist. It squeaks and moves. Whew. Relief. He clamps the pliers on the other hose coupling. It's a little stubborn, too, but he gets it off.

The man tells me that the installation will take about fifteen minutes. I can come back then. I return to our apartment and doodle around on the computer for what feels like fifteen minutes. I go out to see how they're doing. The other guy is a little smaller, but he's still a big guy. Just the two of them would provide significant defense in a football game. What's it like being that big? I've always been rather small. Not real small. Not Mickey Rooney small. Bob Dylan small.

The first thing I encounter is a foul stench. The carpet has a large water stain with bits of detritus lying scattered about. It looks like someone vomited. The bigger of the two men tell me that as they were lifting the old washer out it had stagnant water in it which spilled out of the hose. I wonder why they didn't check for that first. I wait for them to offer to clean it up. They don't. They advise me on how to clean it up. The new washer, at least, is fully installed. One of them starts it up and it works fine.

Unfortunately, since the floor is uneven, and there is a depression in the back, there is no surface for the rear leg of the machine. The machine wobbles. That's no good. The larger of the two delivery guys tries to see if the legs are adjustable. They're not. As he struggles with his pliers to get the leg to move, I spot a sock that's been lying in back of the machine since the beginning of time. It's pretty grody. I make a mental note of grabbing it but forget.

The delivery guy gives up and leaves the machine at an angle. It doesn't wobble at an angle. But there's a little table upon which sits bottles of laundry soap and now that little table has to stick out a little more than it did before. Also, I forget about the sock. The sock bugs me.

I go out to sign for the delivery, come back and fill a bucket with water and Spic 'n Span and go to work cleaning up the mess. I scrub it with a brush and dump the used water down the drain in the laundry room. I clean wads of hair and detritus off the grill of the drain with a paper towel and toss it in a trash can.

When I finish, I get dressed for a run and take off. My legs hurt, but the air smells good. The sun is out. I think of something Blaise Pascal said. He said "the least movement is of importance to all nature. The entire ocean is affected by a pebble."

Hallelujah.

The following day, a Saturday, as soon as Roberta comes home from work in the early afternoon and our cat races out to greet her as she checks our mailbox, we have a conversation with the lady who lives upstairs. She hasn't been able to do laundry downstairs for some time. She's gotten into the routine of taking her laundry to a coin-operated laundry. She's reluctant to use the machine because it's sitting at an angle. I tell her about the wobbling. Roberta spots a paintbrush on the floor. I push the washer back and she slides the little paintbrush under the leg. It stabilizes the leg a little, but we need something else. The woman who lives upstairs says she might have something to put under there. While she disappears into her apartment, I get a thin pole that's been sitting on the porch in back of the milkbox (what for I have no idea) and use it to fish the sock out. Roberta picks it up gingerly with her fingers and deposits it in the trashcan.

The woman who lives upstairs comes back down and hands me a little black velour coin purse. Are you sure about this, I ask. This is a really nice coin purse. But she insists. I lift the machine again just a little (it's much heavier than our old machine), just enough for Roberta to get the little coin purse on top of the paintbrush. Then I let the machine down again. The paintbrush-coin purse combo seems to work. It's pretty stable at this point.

On Sunday, I decide to do a load of white clothes. I figure out the settings on the panel and press "start." The machine runs fine. It's a fast machine. When it's done, I go out to move the clothes into the dryer. The machine is still finishing its spin cycle. It sounds like a rocket ship. A good rocket ship, the kind that glides easily through the space-time continuum and responds quickly to emergencies. The kind that makes a little whine, not a complaining whine, but a whine of resolution, a whine of ease and soft landings. The machine trembles a little, but it doesn't wobble. The paintbrush and coin purse seem to be working, supporting that one leg in the rear where lost socks assume their final resting place, collect lint and dirt and disappear for eternity.

On Knowledge

Knowledge is what you know, said Gertrude Stein. What do I know? I know that kaolin is a fine white clay and that black is a color and energy is a capacity for action. I know that true substance develops in solitude and that the nervous system of a crab pursues the architecture of independence. The slide into essence hustles my sense of warranty. It begins with my sense of alienation and mutates into a longing for monarchy. The ooze of existence turns green with semantic lamination. Fluorescence summons the caress of choice. The hives are full. The plays illustrate our lack of control.

I know what gravity is, that is to say, I know that it exists and that I can feel it, I experience it, but I don't know what it is, what makes it work. I know that it has something to do with space and mass and forming stars out of hydrogen and the curvature of the spacetime continuum. I know that it's why coffee doesn't float out of my Beatles mug. I know that it's why I can sit here typing this and that time moves more slowly in a job you hate and that it's notorious for drawing bodies together. I know that it is a fundamental cause of formation, shape, trajectory and methadone treatments.

I know that if I lift an object the object has weight. My body has weight. I know that I can't fight gravity. What would I punch? I've already tried flying. It doesn't work unless I get into an airplane. Flying in an airplane isn't the same as flying by my own willpower like Superman.

I wonder if one day people will be able to take a pill that makes you weightless? Wouldn't that be a gas.

I know that poetry is, in a certain measure, like gravity, since so much of it remains a mystery. Poetry is a form of dark matter. That is to say, it holds the eyes like a hill holds the sky.

The night sky.

I know that friction and hunger are a major cause of war and that gymnasiums are often noisy. I know that there's a certain charming rapport between mohair and oak. I know that I know more than I know is a possibility but I'm fairly certain that I wouldn't know how to court and marry a crocodile without coercion and shoes.

I know that my life has a purpose but I don't know what it is. Or was. Or could be. Or might be. I imagine most people have that same instinctive feeling. But is it instinctive or just necessary? Why else would anyone endure the pains of existence without a little occasional pleasure and a reason, a sense of destiny, a direction. I guess if you've got kids that takes care of that problem. You live for your kids. But if you don't have kids you've got to have faith in something. You can have faith in your own skepticism.

This is a knowledge that mingles well with corollaries and finance. It's difficult to know what motivates people to do what they do. I'm often surprised at how little I know myself. I often do things without knowing why I did them. I do them and then I wonder why, why did I do that? Why did I say that? Why did I fall in love with that sidewalk? Why do I like to pop the bubbles in plastic wrap?

I know that if a nation charges a lot of money for education that it creates a structure of sharp class division and will not hold together as a nation.

I know that if I express an opinion the chances are that more people will disagree than agree with it. How do I know that? I have a lifetime of expressing opinions. My opinions generally piss people off. That's because I took at things from the perspective of art and poetry, the acuity of wild horses or the audacity of froth. I have a difficult time finding the perspective of a more commercial outlook. This makes me highly qualified to rob banks or regret lost opportunities but poorly equipped to manage a rock and roll band or supervise a customer service center at an Ikea store.

I have no idea how TV, radio, computers, electricity, or light work. But I do know how to eat soup with a spoon and build a correspondence with a fellow writer.

I know the meaning of control and try not to lose what little of it I have within my possession.

I know the joys of possession also invite misery.

I know that Neil Young was born in Canada and that B minor is a sad chord.

Don't ask me about relationships. I wouldn't know where to begin.

I would begin with a thermometer. And end with a sigh.

Directions

Gas stations fascinate me. Especially the ones that actually work on cars. Meechanics who put them up on hydraulic lifts and get under them with ratchets and screwdrivers and stare up into the complexities of gaskets and grease. The ones in which a bell rings when your car passes over a hose. Do they even exist anymore? Most of the gas stations now have minimarts, candy and bottled water and girlie magazines. They don't work on cars. They just offer gas. It's the ones with mechanics and penlights that I like. The ones with an ambiance of grease and gears, voltage and definition. Those stations. The ones in which everything is brisk. Everything is vivid. Everything is loud and determined. The smells are strong. The camaraderie is strong. The exchanges are strong. Discernments are made. Things are fixed. That's what's so fantastic about these places: things get fixed.

Working on a car is a full immersion. Each car is a canto in a long poem which is the highway.

I've always liked cars. This is a difficult thing to admit when so many species are dying and floods are destroying communities due to catastrophic climate change. We've left the Holocene and entered a new geologic epoch, one in which a mass extinction event is in progress.

I grew up with cars. Everybody had a car. Everybody needed a car. It's the way the society is built. It's built around cars. It's only been very recently that some cities, such as Bordeaux in France, have begun prohibiting cars from their downtown streets.

Having a car as a kid meant freedom. You had a way to get out of the house and stay out of the house until you got your own house.

It remains a good feeling. That feeling that I can get into a machine and cover huge distances and within hours find myself in an utterly new region with different cities and different climates and topographies. I can get up and get in the car and go to Cedar Rapids, Iowa. Or Winnemucca, Nevada. It would take 33 hours to drive to San Antonio, Texas. Twenty-four to get to Minneapolis, Minnesota, the city where I first entered this world and spent my early childhood.

No one feels trapped when they have a car. The freedom might be illusory, but it's a compelling sensation, provided you've got enough money for gas, and everything is working.

Having a direction is crucial. It's a way to inhabit space. Space is terrifying without a direction. The dizziness of freedom, to quote Kierkegaard. That's what raw, bare space is all about: the dizziness of freedom. Having a direction takes the edge off.

A direction doesn't have to be geographical, it can be mental, spiritual or intellectual. Having the freedom to change your idea about something or alter your attitude is terrific. But nothing beats having a destination in physical space. A greasy spoon in Tenino, Washington, or Elysium Mons on Mars.

It's wonderful to get into a car, start the engine, crank the wheel and head out to some location.

Time has direction. I can only move forward through time. Time has the appearance of moving forward. I can't make a U-turn and go the other way. Return to my youth. I can only age. Acquire more wrinkles. Acquire more wisdom. Is wisdom a place? Yes, I believe it is. It doesn't have a border, but it does have skills and stationary.

Direction doesn't crackle, hover, or leak. It's a phenomenon, not an object. An airplane can have multiple directions but no immanent transcendence. That is to say, it can have immanent transcendence, but you're going to have to look for it. You can't locate it on a radar screen.

Direction is a component of space. We're seduced into space by direction. Direction is how we experience space. Without direction, space would be horrifying.

I have different moods for different directions. Going east makes me happy. Going west makes me earnest. Going south makes me obstinate. Going north makes me impulsive and sad.

The best feeling is to be heading south to California on a sunny day in June.

The most humbling and exalting is to stand under the stars in Long Beach, Washington. The ocean moves in and flops down on the sand and retreats with that funny hissing sound. And up there, in the sky, gazillions of stars that shine with an ancient light, light that has taken millions of years to reach your eyes.

Metaphysics as a Form of Jungle Gym

The time may have finally come to release language from the leash of common speech and allow it to become a wave on the ocean. Let it roll. Let it swell. Let it float something. Let it reach some island, some continent, some atoll, some isthmus, and crash on the sand.

Dwelling in language isn't healthy. Dwelling in thought isn't healthy. But I do it. I do it anyway. All this makes difficult thinking. I don't know what to think. Until I start thinking. And then it's too late. I'm already thinking.

I don't pretend to be anything I'm not. I'm not a detergent. I'm not a flag or a hermit thrush. I express myself differently. I express myself with algae and barometric pressure. I sparkle with solitude. I like things that require a little reflection to understand them. I never whisper. Whispering isn't my deal. I don't like to shout much either.

I do like words. Words like pearls. Pearls of sweat. Pearls of rain.

Also, car bumpers, though you rarely see them anymore. Chrome bumpers. Not plastic or rubber bumpers. The bumpers you used to see on Chryslers and Fords from the fifties. Red convertibles with fins. Denim blue '55 Chevy pickup with a V8 and flames.

Most of the time I'm just happy to drift. The field is open. Anything can happen.

There's a book on the shelf with a golden spine searching for paradise. *Being and Nothingness* by Jean Paul Sartre. *Lectures in America* by Gertrude Stein. *The Book of Disquiet* by Fernando Pessoa.

Nothing in this world gives itself completely. You've got to share in its existence. It's got to be perceived. Perception doesn't always come easy.

Take clouds. They never stay the same. And eventually it's not even a cloud anymore. It's rain. It's a river. It's an ocean. It's blood. It's soup. It's a hot shower in Grayland, Washington.

Bats fly out of a cave. It's twilight. I rinse out a bottle of dish soap and toss it in the recycling bag and wonder how long it's going to take for all those bubbles to disappear.

Hope is an odd emotion. It's based on an expectation that the future will bring a more favorable circumstance. It's easier just to accept disappointment before it gets here. That way, if something good does happen, it will be delightfully unexpected.

Expect the unexpected. That's my advice.

Is the universe an essentially moral or virtuous place? I don't think so, no. But that's one opinion. And I happen to be biased. I live here.

Is the universe even a place? Is it a place or a being? Is it a jungle gym or a pomegranate?

Whatever paradise is, there aren't any jobs there. Nobody needs a job in paradise. That's what makes it paradise.

What else can I say? The forest is chirping and calm. Why make a principle out of living? There is no principle to living outside of eating and reproducing. What can you say of those who choose not to reproduce? Did they waste everyone's time?

There's no instruction manual for living. You just live. Life lets you know what it wants. Nature provides you with a body. The body wants food and sex. Most of one's life is spent trying to obtain food and sex. In one's later years, it pretty much comes down to food, which is a blessing.

As soon as a philosophy develops, it wants to impose its principles on the world. It wants to remake the world in its own image. Hence, plywood and concrete. Dripstone, gyroscopes, and Queen Anne's lace.

The best philosophy is the one that provides you with cushions.

This is an ancient story: as soon as a philosophy begins to believe in itself, it starts to walk around taking notes and making illustrations. Good microscopes may be obtained at reasonable rates. Abstractions expand into cots.

Every time I put words in a sentence they do this: they begin glue and outlines. Grammar is a muscle. It has a natural tendency to lift things, stretch things, pull things, push things, elongate into beads and spatulas. Sooner or later a philosophy develops. And then what?

You come full circle. You reach that point where language must be released from common speech and become a diversion of ghosts and antiques. Send it on its way. Go, language, and find pleasure in dyes and wheels. Find a fence and jump it. Animate puppets and hammers. Write a letter to Frank O'Hara in the afterlife. I know he's up there. He, too, let his language go. And here it is, indulging the eyes in arguments of mint, finding blood awkward, finding bones heavy, finding a thesis in everything.

The Matter of the Balcony Railing

There's been a lot of talk about the balcony railing lately. Is it up to code? Does it have a soul? What secrets does it hold? Does it have reality? Does it have anyone to blame but itself? What are we to do with it? Why does it have to appear at all? Personally, I don't really care. It's not our balcony. But as an external feature of the building we are to share in its fate and responsibility. In philosophy, this is called the problem of identity over time, or the doctrine of preformation. You may remember the balcony scene from Romeo and Juliet. Well, this has nothing to do with that. This is an HOA situation. I feel the slow crackle of metamorphism. This is called hydrothermal alternation. I feel the clutch of the sublime when I say this. There is a balcony in all of us that develops by rumination. It becomes lost in its arabesques. Though perhaps it may be more accurate to say that it comes to itself in its arabesques. It honors the élan of its own extravagance.

This is what gives the balcony railing its humor of increasing subtlety, of understatement and overstatement, of empirical dance and dynastic abstractness. Whenever I'm feeling parenthetical it helps to think of something prominent and wet. I think of the balcony railing. Its lucidity and inertia. The convivial curves of its filigree. There's a certain implication involved in making an appeal to the vitality of carrots. It is, after all, a balcony railing under discussion here and not a catwalk. If this were a catwalk rather than a railing, I might mention decimals, or pylons. There are intermediates in protein metabolism that will serve as motivational tinfoil. Probable impossibilities are to be preferred to improbable possibilities, said Aristotle. But did Aristotle have a balcony? Did Aristotle cook hamburger on an open grill? Did Aristotle own a single spatula? It is enough that the balcony railing strikes the eyes of the passerby with eloquence. Everything else is morality. No one knows what a belief is. No one knows what a truth is. We just go on pretending that the balcony railing has all the answers. And open our books and read.

Ragwort and Rattlepod

Pain is ceremonious as a funeral procession. I'm not entirely sure who or what to follow into the underworld. I'm not sure I want to visit the underworld. It is said that if one looks long enough in the mirror one will see death. What I see is a face with deepening creases and wrinkles. Bags under the eyes. A wattle under the chin. All you need is love, sang the Beatles, and they were right, of course. But it's harder than one might think to go around in one's mind without getting tangled up in worries and imagine that a feeling of love (I know this is vague, but bear with me) will remedy the situation. The situation being the human condition. In a word: angst. What a great word, angst. It sounds like what it means. A profound aching that penetrates to the bone. A bundle of anxieties, fears, dread, premonitions, conflicts, remorse and dilemmas, all of which begin as soon as cognition begins. As soon as we are brought into this world still covered with blood and slime and open our eyes. The stark light of reality vibrates in the nerves like electricity humming through the high-voltage cables of a transformer station.

It's never-ending, a Möbius loop of perplexities and anguish.

I'm sorry if this is a bummer. But I've chosen pain as my topic and feel a certain responsibility to stick with it.

Thinking is synonymous with apprehension. I think that goes for all people, but since I'm me, and speaking from my point of view, I'd have to say the situation merits special attention.

My mental life is ensnarled with pointless obsessions. This is my brain (picture a sponge). This is my brain on words (picture a sponge dripping words). It's a jungle in there. Tangles of jackalberry, spider lilies, and mangosteen share precious skull space with prickly lettuce, poor-man's spinach, and the Agenbite of Inwit.

Is the Cretaceous over? Not in my head it's not.

Sometimes you can find redemption in a hot dog. It's the food of youth. People eat hot dogs when they're having fun. Put mustard on it. See if it smells of impertinence. If it smells of impertinence, it's a good hot dog. If it doesn't, you might prefer a baked potato.

Pain is rarely this ambiguous. But sometimes yeah, sometimes pain can emit a pagan stubble. The sky murmurs winches and pulleys. Consciousness creates chemicals never before seen on TV. And so goes a skeleton of numbers, another face in the asphalt.

It's confusing as hell. Where did this pain come from? What's it doing bothering me? Why me?

Pain isn't choosey. Pain is as democratic as things get. Apart from thinking. Which is cerebral and sparkly.

Each thought is a fetus in your head. Calendars are shifts in temperature. Pain is pure sorcery. I watched some once roam around a ripple of transparency. It made me feel dribbled, as if existing had to do with everything, including fucking one another. The best way out of this nonsense is to sit down and open a book.

The paper hovers above an emotion constructed out of words. This is what happens in a marriage between emotion and darkness. It's written in my face. Nouns stick to my body like refrigerator magnets. Verbs are more difficult. You have to do them. Perform them. Argue with a forehead. Eat. Sleep. Blow glass.

If you act like a clarinet expect gold and copper. Imagine it's raining on a tank. The men inside are playing cards. That's my definition of lungs. Another is streams of air getting sculpted into words. That's my idea of thinking. The bump bump bump of the beating heart.

Most pains are exquisite. Easy to understand. Easy to resolve. Take your finger out of the fire. Crawl to the lodge and cry for help.

Emotional pain is a little different. It's a dribble of sensation. The drawers jingle with habit. We evade the pain we glaze with our fancy glass.

Outdoors is different. Here I sit as always with clouds floating out of my head. There is so much to describe. When it comes to emotional pain, I rarely feel one singular emotion. It's usually a blend. Grief mixed with fear, fear mixed with gloom, gloom mixed with foreboding. It's often difficult to identify all the nuances in a particular feeling. Conflicts churn in a confusion of color and shape. It hurts my head to have all that shit going on in there. Like Bob Dylan once sang in a song, "there must be some kind of way out of here."

It sometimes happens that a word will assume a quality similar to Saturday. There's a nakedness that happens on Saturday. That's all I know.

Wanting immediate relief is a reason people seek remedy in drugs. It works, but only for a time. When the drugs leave, you feel worse. You have to take more drugs.

You need more drugs to feel the effect of the drugs. It's a vicious circle.

Who designed this universe, anyway?

Words smell of orchids and moss. Light glued together with eyes. Life is sticky with its assumptions, this obsession with gold, this water to twist.

Pain hangs from the lip of a jackhammer like a vegetable.

Fighting a feeling results in making the feeling worse. The more you struggle to resolve an issue, wriggle your way out of it, the tighter it squeezes. The squid gets carried away in a piece of language. The closet pauses long enough to show you Norway. It feels unnatural for a day, then Mick Jagger is dancing in your bathroom.

It's better to make friends with a pain. Take it for walks. Buy it clothes. Enroll it in school.

If the pain is a vague disquiet, I'll try to listen to what it has to say. Often, the message is garbled, like static from outer space.

If the feeling is broken, I'll try to repair it. If I'm going to have a pain, I want it to work properly. A malfunctioning pain is a waste of time and money. If there's a landfill for broken feelings, take it there. You'll see mountains of broken feelings. Seagulls wheeling above, scree! scree! scree!

If I feel powerless to give the feeling what it wants—ten million dollars, a jet, a signed copy of *A Movable Feast*—I'll look for parables. Parables are little stories that provide insight. Insight is to pain what foresight is to hindsight. A sufficient amount of foresight takes the bite out of hindsight. Insight mellows the fury of pain. Insight transmutes pain into wisdom.

None of my insights come easily. I have to strain to find the meaning of a particular pain, and even then I'm more liable to get entangled in it, cut by its thorns. Waves of rumination break against the rocks of a giant opacity.

I'm not a magician. I can't create a storm by which to wreak my vengeance on all the people that have wronged me. I don't live on an island with an obedient daughter and a grumbling monster who brings in the wood. I'm not that guy. But I do have a lot of books. And a lot of the books have something to say about the lessons of pain.

"Pain has an element of blank," says Emily Dickinson.

> It cannot recollect
> When it began, or if there were
> A day when it was not.
>
> It has no future but itself,
> Its infinite realms contain
> Its past, enlightened to perceive
> New periods of pain.

And then, of course, there's Hamlet. This is a guy who seemed to wallow in his pain. He created great speeches out of it. You have to marvel at the idea that one of the most eloquent pieces of literary work in the English language is a contemplation of suicide. "Tis a consummation devoutly to be wished," says Hamlet. Then checks himself: "…in that sleep of death what dreams may come?" Why else put up with the pangs of oppression, the tedium of a shit job, the ordeals of homelessness, the humiliations and hurt of rejection, were it not for "the dread of something after death?" "Thus conscience does make cowards of us all."

Which is one way to look at it.

Another is to live as vigorously as you can and find what pleasures you can to balance it out, mingle the consonants of pain with the vowels of consolation. Talk to your pain. Learn from it. Don't fight it. Don't debate it. Treat it like a prayer. Because maybe that's what pain ultimately is: a prayer.

Sillybrations

Who would've guessed? Today (March 14th) is Fill Our Stapler Day. But I don't have a stapler. I'm very sad. However, I am looking forward to As Young as You Feel Day, which happens on March 22nd.

How young do I feel? I feel like I'm eighteen, but with a full blown case of BPH (benign prostatic hyperplasia) and too many wrinkles. You might think I'm sharing too much information, but today (March 16th) is also Freedom of Information Day. I have a lot more information to share, but for now I want to express how much I'm looking forward to next year's Extraterrestrial Culture Day (February 9th), Don't Cry Over Spilt Milk Day (February 11th), and Absinthe Day (March 8th). Those days managed to slip by without participating in an extraterrestrial event, drinking absinthe, or crying over spilled milk. To be honest, I didn't spill any milk. I don't like milk, nor do I drink absinthe, but I will keep that to myself on February 11th and show humble respect to those who try not to weep over spilled milk, or cast a sympathetic eye on the drunken stupor of the absinthe drinkers while I, substituting one beverage for another, absent-mindedly sip a cream soda.

Ice cream soda day will have my full attention on June 20th.

Soon also to be celebrated are Awkward Moments Day (March 18th), School Nurse Day (May 7th), Change A Light Day (October 2nd), Face Your Fears Day (October 11th) and—a personal favorite—Zero Tasking Day (November 6th).

The list is endless. There's probably even an Endless List Day.

Let us enlist in a celebration of Endless List Day.

Is there a Celebration Day Celebration? A Celebration of celebrations?

Over the years I've celebrated weddings, retirements, elections, and time itself (New Year's).

My favorite celebration is Gazing Out of the Window Day. I just invented it. I'm doing it. I'm gazing out of the window. It's a celebration. I can feel it. I can feel a fleeting euphoria pass through me and come out the other side as a feeling of gratified participation in the pageantry of life. Patches of sunlight, somebody's head, a big gray cat. Gazing out of the window is special. It should be honored with idleness, rumination, and rhesus monkeys.

Now that I've resumed gazing at the computer screen I must repurpose my activity. I will call this Gazing at the Computer Screen Day.

Why 'day'? Why is there never a celebration at night? There are, of course, celebrations that occur at night. But no one says "today is Plum Pudding Night." Or, "Tonight is National Popcorn Night."

Is there a celebration for night? For sleep? For late night movies? For popcorn?

National Popcorn Day occurs January 19th. I'm making my costume now. Popcorn shirt, popcorn pants, popcorn shoes. There will be a re-enactment of the birth of popcorn. The Popcorn Bird will descend from the Popcorn Sky and lay hundreds of Popcorn Eggs in the Popcorn Tree. All the eggs will hatch at once: pop! pop! pop! pop! pop! and hundreds of Popcorn Birds will begin begging for popcorn.

If you happened to be reading this on January 19th, have a Happy Popcorn Day. Until then, may you celebrate whatever day it happens to be, including Bring Your Manners to Work Day (September 2nd), Iguana Awareness Day (September 8th), or Origami Day (November 11th).

Or not.

Tie one on on National Knot Day. Is there a National Knot Day? If not, I will be undone.

Aerial Ikebana

I decide, at around 12:30 p.m., to cut loose of the computer and go for a long walk. My usual preference is to go for a run, but my legs are shot. They need a rest. All the experts on the subject affirm that walking helps the runner's legs heal because it's a low-impact exercise that stimulates the blood and loosens tight muscles. Well, we'll see.

I listen to "Jumpin' Jack Flash" on YouTube while changing into my running clothes. When it's over, I click it off. Van Gogh's bedroom in Arles appears on the desktop background. I've always loved this painting. The two straw chairs, the lush red blanket poking over the edge of the bed, the bright yellow window panes framed in green, the planks of the bare wooden floor partitioned by various lines of green, the little table with the blue pitcher and bowl, a towel hanging from a peg on the wall. The various shades of blue on the walls, the bright yellow pillows and sheet and solid wooden bed, soft as mousse yet secure as a mountain. It's a small room with a feeling of coziness and jubilation. Isolated and private, but connected, in an amiable umbilical of implied domestic charm, with the larger life of Arles outside its windows.

I get outside. It really is warm. I can feel the heat of the sun on my skin, but I don't believe it. I cannot believe my skin. I'm so accustomed to cold and damp in Seattle, even in the summer, quite often in the summer, most especially in the summer, that if I feel the heat of summer, a real summer, the blaze of sunlight tingling on my epidermal nerves, I remain incredulous. But it is a most pleasant incredulity.

I'm amazed at the amount of scaffolding I see everywhere. There is a mania for remodeling evident in the neighborhood. No one is happy with what they have. No one is ever satisfied. The quantity of money spent is dizzying. Astronomical amounts of money are lavished on real estate. The gracefully curved I-beams of the steel skeleton under construction on the corner of Highland and 2nd Avenue will be worth five to seven million. The Space Needle will be neatly centered in the main window with its view to the south. This will be the home of a one-percenter.

I feel a cooling breeze as I approach Queen Anne Avenue North and hear the roar of the first Blue Angel, who flies immediately overheard. It strikes how weird it is that a show of military prowess should provide a summer entertainment. It is this way every year: Seafair. The chief entertainment of Seattle's Seafair celebration are the hydroplane races on Lake Washingtion, near Seward Park. That's too far for me to hear, thankfully. But no one can avoid the Blue Angels. They will be dominating the sky for the next several hours.

On Highland, I pass a man singing along with an opera in a silver SUV parked near Gerard Schwartz's old house. Schwartz, Seattle's symphony conductor for 26 years, from 1985 to 2011. I used to pass him on my runs. He'd be out and about weeding, mowing the lawn, or tossing a football with one of his kids. One he was out jump starting a car. I shouted "conducting cars these days, eh." He gave me a look that suggested it wasn't the best of jokes. Maybe he hadn't realized it had been intended as a joke. He'd been besieged by petty disputes and disgruntled musicians in his final days. One can only imagine. The house sold for $3,700,000.

I stop at the Betty Bowen Viewpoint at the very end of Highland Drive to admire the view. I can see Puget Sound, Bainbridge and Vashon and Blake Islands, the Olympic Mountains. A zaftig middle-aged woman to my left also gazes. She looks transported. Her right arm is in a black sling.

I once saw Sam Waterston near this viewpoint. Or at least I think it was Sam Waterston. He sure looked like Sam Waterston. He was gazing out at the Olympics and turned just as I went running by and gave me a broad emotional grin. A Sam Waterston grin. He looked familiar. And then I thought of it a few yards later down the road: Sam Waterston.

On my way to West Blaine Street on 8th Avenue North I pass a Volkswagen "bio car." What's a "bio car," I wonder. I presume it runs on methane or farts or maple syrup or something.

In a large sandbox at the end of Howe Street, a couple sit and draw, totally silent, heavy in concentration.

I get to the always busy and rushing 15th Avenue West, a main arterial connecting lower Queen Anne and downtown Seattle to Ballard. I pass Magnolia Storage, where Roberta and I have a bin full of boxes and books and bric-a-brac. Letters dating back to my adolescent Eocene.

I pass the Brown Bear Car Wash and hear its roar as a black Taurus inches forward on rails. I pass the tentacular sponges dancing and wiggling on a white van for a magazine distributor. I notice the mama bear in the rockery of ferns has three cubs, one of which is smaller than the other two. How did that happen? The bears are, I believe, plastic, but I find this smaller of the cubs puts a strange dent in the continuity of the narrative suggested in this neatly gardened rockery.

I pass a furniture consignment store and notice in the far back of the parking lot some sort of set-up involving Polynesian décor, palm fronds and grass. This is the Psychic Tarot Card Readings site advertised by a small portable fold-up sign on the sidewalk.

I pass Bedrock Industries, glass tile and stone art. I pass a giant billboard for Busch beer with the caption "Head for the Mountains." I pass the Staples where we bought our computer, the Lighthouse Uniform Company, and Builders Hardware & Supply, a big building with a huge array of doorknobs in the window. Nearby is the walk button for the crosswalk. On the other side is

Precision Motor Works and the multi-tiered ramp leading up to the overpass crossing the railroad tracks. I always enjoy running up this ramp. But today I must walk it.

There is a giant gray warship of some kind at Terminal 91, parked next to an equally colossal cruise ship named the Golden Princess. The warship, I discover later, is the USS New Orleans, a high-tech amphibious assault ship which ferries Marines and their equipment to and from war zones. It features two immense pyramidal funnels. The ship is festooned with multi-colored pennants and there are concession stands set up below in the parking lot. The ship must be part of Seafair. And again, I wonder, what's up with the militarism?

I walk the asphalt trail through Myrtle Edwards Park. This has been a bad year for walking the Myrtle Edwards trail. The city is constructing a bridge connecting West Thomas street and lower Queen Anne to the park, which will be great once it's completed, but in the meantime the bicycle lane has been shut down and the runners and walkers must share their trail with bicyclists hurtling past like meteors. There are signs cautioning the bicyclists to go slow and use caution. They do neither. I wonder how many walkers have been ambulanced to Harborview thanks to one of these crazy bicyclists.

I have a theory, which is this: there are neurons in the anus and rectum of bicyclists that become activated when the bicyclist gets his or her ass on a tiny bicycle seat. And since the neurons are asshole neurons, they immediately turn the bicyclist into an asshole.

I see the vapor trail of a Blue Angel to the south, a huge diaphanous loop already in the process of slow summery dissipation, just above the buildings of downtown Seattle. Minutes later, four Blue Angels shoot straight up and arc out, creating a sort of aerial ikebana.

I pass a cluster of bare-torsoed tattooed twenty-somethings sitting in the shade of a tree. One of them calls out, "hey dude, there's a beached whale down there." I stop. He repeats himself. I tell him he's kidding. He says no, it's for real. I go have a look. Below is a small pocket beach. It's feasible a whale could beach itself down there. Whales do come into Puget Sound and on a hot day like today, with all the Seafair hullabaloo and boats on the water, it's completely feasible. I tell the kid I see nothing. He elaborates, talking about how they straddled the creature, and I begin to worry these kids might be a little on the psychopathic side, and that he's going to tell me how they tortured the poor creature. Instead, he proceeds with a far-fetched tale of a fat woman jumping down to the whale from the Space Needle, and I realize these kids are having me on. "Let me guess," I tell them, "you're all part of a creative writing class." One of the men tells me he teaches special ed. Another begins another story I don't really want to hear about some fabulous mythical bird he saw preening itself in a nearby tree. The Blue Angels roar overhead, just a few feet above us, and I use this as an excuse to break off and go my way.

Toward the end of the trail, a booth has been set up for a DJ, who is playing "Because" from the Beatle's

Abbey Road. It's gorgeous. I nearly start crying. I can't believe how beautiful this song is. The lushness of the melody and their voices is stunning. I continue. I stop to gaze down at Mark di Suvero's *Schubert Sonata*, its circular sublimations and metal petals and curves of rusting steel besmirched a little with pigeon dung. A bit further up the gravel trail and I hear the pounding militarism of a hip hop number and see a group of people doing aerobic exercise, following the lead of a young man and woman. The woman thrusts and gyrates. The music is abrasive, aggressive, corporate. It makes me think of vulgar, highly commercialized acts like Madonna and Lady Gaga. It's madly assertive and sluttish all at once. Worlds apart from the lush harmonies of the Beatles.

I stop at Silver Platters and buy two used DVDs: *School of Rock* and *Young Adult*. We've seen both movies at least once. We both really like Jack Black, and Richard Linklater, and were fascinated by the character Charleze Theron played in *Young Adult*, a ghost writer for young adult novels. She's deeply unhappy and her return to the middle-class neighborhood in the small Minnesota town where she grew up is an interesting pilgrimage involving homemade bourbon and a cynical but dauntless character named Matt Freehauf, played by Patton Oswalt, who was maimed and partially disabled after being beaten up by jocks who erroneously assumed he was gay. I like the way hurt and personal injury is expressed in this movie, and the way Theron punctures the smug banality of her high school buddies.

I get home and am surprised, as I am every summer the temperature rises above 80, at how cool and peaceful our apartment remains. Roberta gets home shortly after I shower and she makes hoagie sandwiches and we watch Jack Black get a bunch of 10 year olds to play rock 'n roll.

Essences and Sentences

Can one create a simulacrum of free will?
　No.
　Free will is free will. It is either free, or it is not even will.
　Free will, by itself, is sturdy. It is nascent. It is art. It is warrant. It is a block of thought and water baked into a brick of prose.
　Think of this as a grape. Bursting, as Keats described, on your palate.
　In, of all places, an ode to melancholy.
　Then ask yourself: what sort of life have I led.
　Writing is strangest when it moves through the eyes seeing the world for the first time. This is why I employ black to promote the power of red. Why sorcery overrides the dictates of logic. Why perceptions shine on the page. Why gauze is sometimes in fashion, and sometimes it is not.
　We feel trapped in our own ideas. Dew beaded on the fronds of a fern, the gleam of rails in a train station.

Ink is a medium of the intellect. It is a fluid. It is sometimes black, sometimes blue. Its viscosity allows for expression. But it dries instantly. Allowing for durability. For pipes and canoes and the beckoning of the wilderness.

Pull a shape out of a chair, and you still have a chair. Essence is a sensation. I feel a surge of joy at the very idea of pi.

Europe, on the other hand, is accomplished by thinking. Lips flap, words fly. Spain is described as a luminous feeling. France is described as a story of bulbs and burgundy. England is described as Jimi Hendrix playing Voodoo Child on the Lulu Show.

I wear a mask of turbulent steam not to dissimulate, but to simulate the simmering of galaxies scribbled into space.

Talking fills the vineyards of autumn.

My friend, who are you?

This is my new metaphor: bone. Each personal history has a certain weight. Water reflects the vagaries of thought, and reverie, which is a soft light, a loaf of bread, and a squirrel. Everything of value stems from diversion.

For instance, I love the sound of rain. You can find everything in it. Everything and nothing. Definitions always fall short.

Avoid politics. Consciousness is fueled by amazement. A flight of steps embowered by sycamore.

Forgive me if my fingers infringe on the sanctity of your knees. The clarinet is a parable of valves. Listen to the robins. The world is accelerated by foment. Ronnie

Wood in a beet field painting the sky. Braque, accompanied by Apollinaire, meeting Picasso for the first time. The physics of walking. The hardware of talking.

Distill a participle into a jar of pickles. Consider this an elegy of glass. Surly women. The smell of sex.

Les Demoiselles D'Avignon.

Is there a force strong enough to stop war? Such is my vision. My movements are telegraphic. A coherent incoherence. And so we danced all night. And the war came to an end. In our minds.

This is my knife. Watch as I hurl it. Watch as it bounces down the street. Clink, clink, clink.

No allegory is complete without a winner. Which is why a fight broke out at last night's bingo game.

Fog argues with oak.

Each road is a mental adventure. A memory of silver. A thermometer mutilating winter's stern temperatures.

It is astonishing how crude, vulgar, violent, and materialistic life in the U.S. has become.

The metamorphosis of thought is dramatized by tin.

Or a sweet and bubbly strain of music.

A squirrel sitting on a rock eating a peanut.

Our emotions are faster than pianos. Each river has two shores. The Beatle's *Revolver* plays in a '94 Subaru.

In 2010. And nothing has changed. Except everything. Which was books. And ghosts. And words employed in melody.

Certain things cannot be denied. Especially cemeteries.

I find it strange that no one comments on these things.

I cannot give you a good reason as to why I write. But here is a sentence swarming with shrimp, and here is a polymer in the creation of a protein.

Here is a freshly squeezed Philippine sponge, dripping.

Here is a private thought. It's invisible.

Except on paper, where it ceases to be private, and becomes a passion. An explanation. For the need of decoration. Ornaments and lies. And the little irritations that fill a day. Make it what it is. Or was meant to be.

A circumference. A farm. A declaration of freedom.

I am but a humble piece of meat, studying the curls of your hair.

What can a goldfish tell us of reality? Are we truly the inheritors of something sublime? Or merely deluded?

I cannot help but notice that our planet is dying. Even the dinosaurs weren't this savage. They merely left a legacy of bones. Imprints and shells.

What will we leave behind?

Ideas of free will? How will they take shape? What form? What essence? What value?

Spars, whispers, paths. All of it gone. Gas stations included.

Walking and Dancing

During a Q&A at the Harvard Exit several years back the actress Karen Black said, with fervent conviction, that the arts were all about communication. Something in that statement bothered me. It's taken years of mulling that statement over to come up with an analogy I can only wish I'd had the presence of mind to present to her at the time. The analogy has to do with walking and dancing. Walking is usually goal-oriented; we walk home, walk to work, walk a dog, walk to a store. Dance, on the other hand, is not goal-oriented. Dance is simply a delight and exploration of movement itself. So what does that say about communication? Communication is goal-oriented. Its mission is to dispense information, instructions, advice, knowledge, propaganda. Most poetry, the kind of poetry that ends up in cornball "best of" anthologies, or recited on NPR by people like Garrison Keillor, do communicate. The poetry is anecdotal and one-dimensional. It's unabashedly goal oriented, a form of walking. There's a pragmatic sense of delivering wisdom, a charged emotion, an insight, a pithy saying for a calendar. But the more recondite poetry, what does that do? It's more like dance: it revels in words. It's not goal oriented. There's nothing pragmatic about it. If wisdom is to be found, it tends to be accidental, and something the reader has read into it. How might've Karen Black responded to this? How embellished this thought?

Moss

There is a time in the afternoon in deep winter when, if the sun is out, the moss on the surface of the balustrade of Queen Anne boulevard goes into high definition and turns iridescent. It is green beyond belief. It looks like a thick carpet, but with a lumpy, irregular surface and little whiskery shoots bristling among the prominences.

Moss is ubiquitous in the northwest. It covers everything. Roofs, walls, trees, gables, gallstones, gargoyles, garages. Moss loves moisture. And there is plenty of moisture in the northwest. The northwest is to moisture what mecca is to Islam. What ovals are to eggs. What monuments are to wars. What shadows are to light. If moss were a form of credit, it would be the International Exchange of the global credit default swap swamp.

But moss is insistently, consistently moss. That's what makes moss, moss. To compare moss to something else is to lose the mossness of moss.

I am charmed by moss. It is original and massive. It spreads like a superstition throughout all the balustrades and coffeehouse bricks of the dripping northwest.

It feels like an animal. If you brush your hand over its surface very softly, it feels remarkably like fur.

If you get lost in the woods, look for moss on one side of the tree. That will be the north side of the tree. North, where the sunlight is blocked. Moss likes shade. It feeds on dark things, like the necropolis of the Etruscans.

The moss growing on the balustrade of 7th Avenue West seems anomalous in its obvious appreciation of sunlight. Is it a species apart from the usual moss that carpets the shady nooks and recesses of the Pacific Northwest?

Yesterday, I had to stop by the balustrade to tie my shoelace. I was doing my usual afternoon run and was moist beneath my running clothes. I felt the cold immediately. I raised my leg and positioned my foot in the hole of the balustrade. A sharp winter breeze blew through the hole. I looked to the west where the sun was already beginning to set. The light was sharp. The moss stood out in high relief, attracting my attention to the spot where I had rested my gloves, black wool against a patch of green iridescence. It felt like an elegy. A sweet rag of holy fuzz marking the end of a day in early January.

Ruskin and Rust

John Ruskin would have liked our windshield wiper. The one to the right, on the passenger side. It has begun to rust. There is a patch of rust on the hinge; it is a bright, lucent cinnamon. It catches the eye, and one wonders if it is beautiful or not. If it is something requiring repair. You decide it is beautiful and does not require repair.

Ruskin liked rust. This is what my wife Roberta told me. She showed me the passage in the book she is reading, *On Art And Life:*

You all probably know that the ochreous stain, which, perhaps, is often thought to spoil the basin of your spring, is iron in a state of rust: and when you see rusty iron in other places you generally think, not only that it spoils the places it stains, but that it is spoiled itself—that rusty iron is spoiled iron. For most of our uses it generally is so; and because we cannot use a rusty knife or razor so well as a polished one, we suppose it to be a great defect in iron that it is subject to rust. But not at all. On the contrary, the most perfect and useful state of it is that ochreous stain; and therefore it is endowed with so ready a disposition to get itself into that state. It is not a fault in the iron, but a virtue, to be so fond of getting rusted, for in that condition it fulfills its most important functions in the universe, and most kindly duties to mankind. Nay, in a certain sense, and almost a literal one, we may say that iron rusted is Living; but when pure or polished, Dead.

She was right. Ruskin really liked rust. Liked it because it awakened reveries of dissonance and paradox, deviation and irony.

Which brings me to life. What is life? Here is a paragraph swimming with words. Teeming with words. Does this mean the paragraph is alive? Yes, it certainly does. I don't know how television works but I do know how paragraphs work. They boil the mind like water. They open like drawers. They grow into willows at the cemetery. Just as the stars pause before dawn. And French happens to a sumac. And four women bathe in a river in West Africa singing songs to keep the crocodiles at bay.

Is consciousness a product of emotion? Is consciousness rust, or stainless steel?

Consciousness is a personality clinging to one's being. Picasso sitting in a chair. Swimming and silver. And most certainly rust.

Intervals

When philosopher and author Yannick Haenel found himself unemployed, unable to pay the rent on his Paris apartment and eventually evicted, he began living in his car. It was 3:00 o'clock on a Sunday afternoon and the car was parked by the sidewalk. Cherry petals twirled in the air and came to rest on his windshield. It was his good fortune that the car was parked on the rue de la Chine, one of the last Parisian streets that didn't charge for parking. He had in his possession three cardboard boxes packed with laundry and books. The apartment had been furnished. The car belonged to a friend in Africa who'd not yet made plans to return. He had no idea what to do. He had no other alternative but to sit in his car and muse on the vagaries of life. He was outside the protective walls of daily stability. The odd thing was, he felt serene. He felt a peculiar sense of well-being. This was a new chapter in his life. A life which suddenly felt delightfully disengaged, free of the usual domestic hassles and responsibilities.

It was, at first, an odd sensation, being behind the wheel of a car, pedestrians walking by paying no attention, but with nowhere to go, no reason to start the engine. Just sit. Sit and gaze. Sit and think. Sit and muse. It was like falling into a hole.

But the hole he dropped through landed him in what he referred to as an interval, a feeling combined of joy and what the French call *déchirure,* of being ripped, wrenched, torn. It is, he says, hard to describe. It's one of those feelings that elude definition and is a mixture of contradictory emotions, but more than that, it extends meaning into the void.

Yannick turned the key and the radio came on. It was the news concerning the national election for a new president. It did not matter in the least to him. He had long since begun to feel disconnected from politics. I know the feeling. After having voted for Obama in the first election, and watched as he pursued policies even more violent and diabolical than those of the Bush administration, I realized that George Carlin had been right. Voting is useless.

France and America are not that different, at least not when it comes to politics. There is the same corruption, the same empty platitudes delivered to appease the populace, the same deceptions, the same elite class running things for the banks and corporations.

The least link connecting him to society felt absurd, remarked Yannick. Amen, say I.

In music, an interval refers to the distance in pitch between two notes, which is expressed in terms of the number of notes of the diatonic scale which they comprise (e.g. third, fifth, ninth) and a qualifying word (perfect, imperfect, major, minor, augmented, or diminished).

As Yannick noted (so to speak), there are intervals in life as well. Spaces between the major notes of our histories, our engagements, our chronologies that may be described as those perfect or imperfect, major or minor, augmented or diminished spaces where the theme goes somewhat awry, where the sound turns strange, chromatic, and a little uncertain. Diana Raffman, author of *Language, Music, and Mind*, calls it "nuance ineffability." Music is structural, it has a grammar and proposes a meaning. When something is felt or heard that violates our semantic expectations and as such cannot be explained in language, it is a nuance ineffability. We recognize the melody and rhythm but the pitch deviations may elude our notice because they're not entirely within the range of our hearing. We hear minor sixths and perfect fourths, but the more fine-grained discriminations escape any categorical identification. They're relational. Their existence is purely imagined, or felt. They're anisochronous, outside the time interval separating any two corresponding transitions and not related to the time interval separating any other two transitions. Tonal musical stimuli are heard against the backdrop of a richly structured, albeit pliant, mental grid.

They exist as a kind of evanescent aureole scintillating around the structural organization of the work.

Such intervals occur in my life when my usual patterns are disrupted and I'm waiting for something, a plane flight, a bus, a dentist, a doctor, a train. These are small interludes in which, freed from my general tasks, I have a space in which to daydream or take in phenomena that might otherwise elude my attention.

There have been longer interludes, ones more similar to Yannick Haenel's homeless situation in his car. Long periods of unemployment in which I had nothing to do between appointments or interviews but sit in a car and read or ponder the weightier issues of my life. Existence feels a little more raw on these occasions. There are no daily rituals to encompass or structure our day. Improvisation and spontaneity and openness to new experience are more to the fore.

I experienced a very deep sense of disconnectedness upon graduating from college in 1973. I'd been divorced the previous year, which added to my sense of detachment. I would not characterize it as "footloose and fancy free." It was more like being marooned on an island.

I wasn't entirely homeless. I lived with my father and stepmother for a considerable amount of time, months, in fact, before I found a job and was able to rent a small apartment. I spent long periods in my car at the time. The car itself was not a car of my own choosing but had been given to me by my stepmother. It was a six-cylinder

Dodge dart, silver in color, I continue to wince to this day when I think how poorly I cared for that car. It had been remarkably reliable even though the dismal income my menial job provided did not permit me to finance the kind of care the car—any car—requires. Change the oil, clean the air filter, check the cooling system, etc. Cheap things, I know, but my wages were gulped by rent, food, and (it shames me to confess it) booze.

Drugs make intervals much more interesting, but it is not necessarily something I endorse. Marijuana is legal in Washington, more or less, and I've always perceived that particular drug, which is a plant, as natural and relatively innocuous when it comes to addiction and the health of the body. It's a cheap, relatively benign high, but I never liked marijuana. It always made me feel weirdly claustrophobic, as if I were trapped in myself, underwater. I don't know why it made me feel like I was underwater. This had nothing to do with breathing. It was a sense of being immersed and overwhelmed by social phenomena that I had difficulty comprehending. My general reaction to marijuana was always one of fear and paranoia. Not fun.

I find that it is in the nature of the interval itself to bring about an altered state of consciousness. Travel does that. I've always noted my mind is more active when I travel. Novelty is ever present and one's responsibilities are far away and tucked away at home.

Coffeehouses make a nice location for those temporary disruptions in one's activities, though I enjoy them far less now that everyone is gazing into smartphones and laptop computers. I feel offended by it. I know it's not rational, but there it is: I feel violated.

Perhaps it is my life-long devotion to books, to magazines and newspapers, to the print media in general. What offends me is the mental laziness of people and the fickleness of their attention, the degradation of their absorption, their scrutiny and thinking. I feel the grid tightening. I see a corporate group-think running rampant and taking root. I could easily become a Carrie Nation of the coffeehouse, tearing people's digital toys and apparatus out of their hands and crushing them with my feet.

The world's intervals are fast disappearing. Time is at a premium. Idleness has acquired a dirty name. Who remembers Walt Whitman's lovely declaration: I loaf and invite my soul, I lean and loaf at my ease observing a spear of summer grass.

Now there was a man of intervals.

Song Brocade

There is a song of silk called Song Brocade. Brocade during China's Song Dynasty put its emphasis on liveliness and color. Eye candy. Brilliant colors, exquisite patterns, a supple and resistant texture. Expensive and heavy, it wasn't suitable for clothing, but had about it the bulk of sunlight. Its patterns dreamed in the woof and warp of graceful dexterity. It created a geometry of flowers and animals, clouds and dragons. Colors were divided into three categories: harmonic colors based on yellow, harmonic colors based on grey, contrasting colors based on red, green and orange. One imagines the sound of the looms as a clatter and a fabulous sincerity of effort, as if a kind of surgery were being performed, or consciousness loomed from wood.

Evergreens swayed by the Yangtze. Rain puddled in the hollows of flagstone. Sandalwood incense brocaded the quiet air in the Temple of the Loom Spirit.

Jĭn is Chinese for 'brocade.' As in:

水中的涟漪在阳光的照射下似锦缎布匹一样光滑油亮。

"The ripples on the water are as smooth and bright as a brocade under the sunshine."

English brocade comes from Italian *broccato*, meaning "embossed cloth," *panno in rilievo*, and has the same root as the word "broccoli." In Italian, the verb *broccare* means "to stud, to set with nails," which comes from *brocco*, small nail, which in turn comes from Latin *broccus*, "projecting, or pointed." These words put my mind in relation with sharp things that poke, that are meant to penetrate cloth, and raise threads to a condition of legibility, in the same way that a pen might measle paper with the needlepoint of life, transcendence, transformation, the private soliloquys that whistle us into tumults of elaborated thought.

Brocade occurs in writing when the intent is to make of language a tool of precision, a spigot of points, needles, gold, silver, silk, nebulous desires, communion, incarnations of text and texture, the energy of signs, of prophecies and fables, roots and origins, buffalo and pearls, ecstasies and convulsions, fabulous voyages, marriage propositions, death in the family, epiphanies, exotic wildlife, savage ruminations, mythological creatures, worms and Turkish harems.

Themes are never truly singular but a matter of warps and woofs, a cross-weaving of contraries, an attempt to bring meaning and pattern to the arbitrariness of signs and experience. Mocassins and prayers mix with picks and ribbons, dragons and glowworms, glissandos of conscioussness resonant as Zhejiang gongs. The impulsion of blood the refinement of orchids. Time and gravity are cross-weavings of woof and warp in the loom of space. The semantic froth of allegory floats the creak and groan of speculative wood. The delicacy of sand reveals ripples of wind. There is a weaving of everything that stretches as far as the grandeur of time in infinity's phantasmal silk.

Tinfoil

If language hadn't yet been invented what sound would you make to represent the sun? Me, I'd make a sound like a conifer.

Or a conjecture. Or a contusion. Convulsions of flame heating a planet of hair salons.

You have to be careful when making sounds. Sometimes a sound will golf its way through Switzerland and bend the air into a paragraph.

This is that paragraph. You can see it sparkling beneath these words. The arabesques are spinning in eternal glory. The eggs are crackling. The words are swarming with sound. Thousands of sounds. Naked sounds. Folds and sleeves and hoses of sound.

Awakened syllables blossom like soap. Science is unofficially stippled to look like a wrinkled afternoon. This is as empirical as things get around here. Even the raspberries thunder with red. Vermillion sorrows marry the vowels of night and by early morning the weather has turned plump and pneumatic.

If language hadn't been invented I wouldn't be able to say apple and mean it. Whipped cream would idle in ineffective oscillation squeezing its potential from a sag in time.

Sometimes I think of kelp and wonder how it happened. How did language happen? Did someone burst into paper while percolating their perceptions in a willow?

Life is often sticky. It's important to stretch. This is why I smell like an earthquake. The submarines are thick with exultation. Diversions transfer throats between coffee breaks. The trapeze is a simple ghost. I would rather effervesce than demand a configuration of spit. I've always liked the way pigment distorts reality. The journey gets bigger and walks in bone. I'm moistened by appliance. I have vascularity. I have needs. I have interactions with hue and experiments that draw crows. Sometimes I'm all emotion and sometimes I have the emotion of a milieu in Nebraska, a pile of hay or a street in Omaha or a gauze hanging in somebody's window.

I can't get out of my fingers unless I open my hand. Therefore, I make a fist and then let it go. If it rains it's not my fault. It's just a vertigo swimming through a dictionary. Hammerheads break into abstraction. The business of thinking gets murky with pulchritude. Would anyone like tea? Whatever happened to that Neal Cassady letter that was supposed to go on auction at Christie's this month? I'm no authority on symbolism, but I must admit that clutching a vowel is totally French. Life is mostly friction. If you feel sublime, raise your hand and a monitor will bring you a whisper of ginger.

How did language get so entangled with the confusion of the emergency room?

Where does it all come from? I mean, everything. Where does everything come from?

I favor the sounds of the glockenspiel. Bell play. Before there was English, there was German. And before there was German, there was air.

    This is how air becomes an architecture. When it is given syllables and exaggeration foreheads bubble out of it. The end result is tinfoil.

Biographies & Acknowledgments

Angela Woodward is the author of the fiction collections *The Human Mind* and *Origins and Other Stories*, and the novels *End of the Fire Cult* and *Natural Wonders*. *Natural Wonders* won the Fiction Collective Two Catherine A. Doctorow Innovative Fiction Prize. *Origins and Other Stories* won the Collagist Magazine prose chapbook competition. *Notes re Erehu* is available from The Artefakta Pamphlets Series, published by Ravenna Press. She lives in Madison, Wisconsin.

Norman Lock's recent books include the poem sequence *In the Time of Rat* (Ravenna Press, 2013) and, from Bellevue Literary Press, *American Meteor* (novel, 2015), *The Boy in His Winter* (novel, 2014), and *Love Among the Particles* (stories, 2013). More at www.normanlock.com. The Cromwell Dixon stories originally appeared in *Pindeldyboz*; "In Envy of Glaciers" and "The Universe of the Body" were published as a chapbook by Mud Luscious Press.

John Olson is the author of numerous books of poetry, essays & prose poetry, including *Larynx Galaxy, Backscatter: New and Selected Poems, Free Stream Velocity* and *Echo Regime*, and four novels, including *Souls of Wind, The Nothing That Is (Ravenna Press), The Seeing Machine*, and *In Advance of the Broken Justy*. *Dada Budapest*, a collection of prose poetry, is forthcoming from Black Widow Press. The author would like to express his gratitude to The *Raven Chronicles* in which "Sillybrations" first appeared and the *Seattle Review of Books* in which "The Matter of the Balcony Railing" first appeared.